The scream came out without her even willing it, but a large, gloved hand slapped over her mouth and practically twisted her head off as it pulled her back. Mary struggled, reaching her arms up over her head and scratching at his ski mask as the attacker pulled her down a set of darkened stairs and planted a fist in her gut.

Doubling over, Mary crumpled to the ground. Something sharp was cutting into her leg, and she could feel the blood spreading out over her skin, sticking to her tights. It was warm, and it brought her to her senses.

Enough to realize that the guy hovering above her was taking off his jacket and going for his zipper.

Don't miss any books in this thrilling new series:

FEARLESS™

Available from POCKET PULSE

FEARLESS™

PAYBACK

FRANCINE PASCAL

POCKET PULSE
New York London Toronto Sydney Singapore

To Alice Elizabeth Wenk

An *Original* Publication *of* POCKET BOOKS

 POCKET PULSE, published by
Pocket Books, a division of Simon & Schuster, Inc.
1230 Avenue of the Americas, New York, NY 10020

 Produced by 17th Street Productions, Inc.
33 West 17th Street
New York, NY 10011

Copyright © 2000 by Francine Pascal

Cover art copyright © 2000 by 17th Street Productions, Inc.
Cover photography by St. Denis. Cover design by Mike Rivilis.

ISBN: 0-671-03946-6

First Pocket Pulse Paperback printing March 2000

10 9 8 7 6 5 4 3 2

Fearless™ is a trademark of Francine Pascal.
POCKET PULSE and colophon are trademarks of Simon & Schuster, Inc.

Printed in the U.S.A.

When

I was five, my baby-sitter, Claire, took me to see my first movie. It was already dark when we came out of the theater, so we started walking toward this big intersection two blocks down where we were sure we could catch a cab.

I was still feeling dazzled by the memory of the music and the big colorful screen when a huge, heavyset man stepped out of a doorway and yanked Claire into the hallway of a nearby brownstone. At that moment I remember being startled and feeling worried about Claire, but I never—not even for a minute—felt scared.

I watched silently as the man shoved a rag into Claire's mouth and began dragging her up the stairs. And instead of running for help like any other kid would have done, I followed the attacker as he dragged Claire, kicking and clawing, up four flights. The guy never even looked around to see where I'd gone.

When we got to the roof, he started tearing off Claire's clothes and fumbling with his belt. Of course, I didn't know what that meant at the time, but I knew fear when I saw it, and it was written all over Claire's face. At that moment I started executing my plan, even though I didn't know I *had* a plan yet.

The guy didn't know what hit him when a spray of gravel pounded his shoulder. And when he turned around to see where it came from, there I stood—my body planted firmly not ten feet from him at the edge of the roof—utterly calm. I swung back my arm and let go another missile shower of biting gravel pellets into his face.

Cursing, he leaped to his feet and charged at me, but just as he lunged, I ducked and rolled out of his way. A nanosecond later all two hundred pounds of him was pitching over the edge of the roof.

He fell four flights to his death.

I can't stand bullies. I can't stand men who think they can push women around. When I can kick some guy's ass for picking on a girl who's usually half his size, it's one of the few times I'm thankful for this strange fear- lessness that I've had since birth. It's one of the few times when I forget to feel like a freak, when I forget to want to be normal—something I can never be. Because no matter how little control I have over my own life and how little courage I have when it comes to Sam, or friend- ship, or letting people in, I *can* do something for the weak one. The loser.

That is when I feel really alive. Because no matter how strong I think I am, the loser always seems to be a lot like me.

What if the
memory suddenly
snapped into
vivid
Technicolor *think*
surround **about**
sound and it
was nothing but **sam**
a big fat . . .
nothing?

"YOU CAN'T POSSIBLY IMAGINE HOW

Weird Weekend

psyched I am that you called," Ed Fargo told Gaia Moore as she stepped out onto the sidewalk in front of her apartment. "I escaped just when my dad was about to retell the retelling of Uncle Alan's story about how he and my mom mooned the nuns on her wedding day. It's like a fish story. Every time someone tells it, Sister Rose suffers a different fate. This time I think she would have had a stroke, and I don't think I could have handled it."

Gaia winced at the sunlight, taking in a deep breath and letting it out slowly. "Right."

Ed sighed. "You're going to have to bring your level of excitement down a notch, G.," he said, a hint of irritation in his voice. "I know you haven't seen me in three days, but your enthusiasm over my presence is making me blush."

"Sorry," Gaia said, stuffing one bare hand into her pocket as she started to walk. The other was clutching a small paper bag she'd picked up off the kitchen counter. "Weird weekend," she mumbled, not sure what, exactly, she should tell him. It had been hard enough when she'd admitted to Ed that she had feelings of, yes, a sexual nature for Sam Moon. Gaia wasn't exactly the heart-to-heart type, and letting anyone in on her secrets went against every fiber in her being. But this had now become more than just a crush. It was bordering on insanity. And Gaia wasn't sure whether telling Ed would help take the weight off her shoulders or merely confirm that she was a first-rate lunatic. Gaia didn't have that many friends to spare. In fact, she only had this one now that Mary was out of the picture. So how much was too much to tell?

It was Sunday morning, and ever since she'd left the hospital on Friday, all Gaia had done was mainline sugar and obsess. Obsess about Sam, think about Sam, dream about Sam. The dream involved kisses that had never really happened. Words that had never really been spoken. They couldn't have been real, no matter how much her muddled, confused brain kept trying to make her believe that they were. Her mind had been sifting random, incongruent images nonstop. Images Gaia couldn't possibly make sense of.

Part of her didn't want to try. What if the memory suddenly snapped into vivid Technicolor surround sound and it was nothing but a big fat . . . nothing? What if nothing at all had happened between her and Sam? Gaia was sure her heart couldn't handle it. As pathetic as it was, she'd rather hold on to the possibility of something perfect than be hit with the reality of nothing much.

Gaia sighed and pushed forward at her usual

breakneck pace, forgetting for a moment that Ed was navigating his wheelchair through the crowd of babbling women surrounding them. She turned around long enough to notice one of the women inadvertently whack his arm with a J. Crew bag. The Christmas shopping rush had officially begun.

The hustle and bustle failed to draw Gaia out of her own confused thoughts as Ed struggled to keep up with her. There were only two things she knew for sure. First, she had been in Sam's room on Thanksgiving. She knew this only because when she was leaving the hospital, a bleary-eyed intern had handed her back her clothes. A T-shirt, a pair of boxers, and a robe. All men's. All with the distinct, musky Sam smell nestled within their folds.

All of which were stashed in a plastic bag, inside a backpack, which was zippered shut and locked with a minilock under her bed. Ella-proof packaging.

The second thing Gaia was completely sure of was that Ella knew something she wasn't telling. That was the part about this whole thing that ate at Gaia like acid through a tin can. Ella knowing more than her. It was just cosmically wrong.

"So what's up?" Ed huffed, catching up to her just before she stepped onto the street, ignoring a solid Don't Walk signal.

"Park," Gaia grunted, holding up the little white bag. "Doughnuts."

"Articulate," Ed commented. "You're quite the cave woman today."

Gaia ignored the comment and kept walking, leading the way into Washington Square Park and dropping onto the first bench she saw. Scowling, she immediately shoved three-quarters of a glazed chocolate doughnut into her mouth. The sticky dough gathered in a lump and lodged halfway down her throat. Where to start?

"Didn't you get enough turkey this weekend?" Ed asked, removing one of the doughnuts from the bag on her lap.

"No turkey," Gaia said while chewing.

"You have to be kidding." Ed picked off a piece of doughnut and popped it into his mouth. "Turkey is the only thing that makes the whole family-gathering debacle bearable."

Gaia shrugged. "I think I might have kissed Sam."

Ed suddenly let out a strangled, choking sound. Gaia turned to him in time to see his eyes fill with water before he doubled over.

That was when the convulsions started.

Ed began to cough like she'd never seen him cough before. He sat gasping, doubled over in his chair, clutching the remaining piece of doughnut so hard, it crumbled into sad little bits and toppled to the ground.

"Ed?"

Gaia started to slap him on the back.

"Ed?"

"I'm okay. I'm okay," Ed said, sitting up and pounding on his chest with his fist. "It just went down the wrong pipe."

Gaia pulled away her arm. Yes, she knew Sam had a girlfriend. And she knew that girlfriend was probably pure evil and her archnemesis to boot. But did that really make the news choke worthy? She hadn't even told Ed the part she'd *really* been worried about. The part about not remembering. The part about not knowing whether she'd really kissed Sam or whether she'd just raved outside his dorm like a semi-concussive psychopath, like Ella had told her she had.

Glancing back at Ed, Gaia noticed he'd finally recovered and was gathering himself to ask her something. By the look on his face, it was probably something she didn't want to answer.

"Okay, okay, spit it out," she snapped. Patience wasn't one of her strengths.

Ed blushed and looked at his feet. "So, uh, did you and Sam . . . do—do anything else?" he stammered.

Gaia could feel herself turning bright red.

"Um. Um. Well, maybe . . . I don't know," she blurted out.

"You don't know," Ed repeated.

"It's a long story," Gaia said, sucking the sticky sugar off her index finger. "I'd had a fight earlier. A bad one.

And I kind of passed out, and I don't remember much. Ella's trying to make me think nothing happened."

"Oh."

Gaia looked down at her whiter-than-white hands and picked at her nonexistent fingernails.

"I haven't heard from him, though," she said, fiddling with a cuticle. "So I guess . . . I guess that means that maybe he doesn't . . . want me."

The look of sadness on Ed's face made her angry. She wasn't telling him this stuff so he could throw her a pity party. She just needed to tell someone she could trust. And she needed to let out the anger. The anger that she couldn't remember. The anger that Ella could. The anger at the idiots who'd beaten her up and made her hit her head so hard that the whole thing was a blur.

"You haven't talked to him at all?" Ed interrupted her thoughts.

Gaia sighed and looked out across the nearly deserted park. People were hurrying through it, their scarves pulled up against the cold. She and Ed were two of only a very few psychos who had stopped to enjoy the frigidity.

"I went to his dorm, but I didn't go in," she said. She didn't go on to say she had stood outside the door of Sam's building for two hours, willing him to come down and find her but never finding the courage to find him.

Ed nodded and followed her gaze to the empty fountain at the center of the park. Suddenly everything looked gray. Everything felt even colder than it was. She wanted Ed to tell her that everything was going to be okay. That Sam would get in touch with her. That it would all work out.

But Ed seemed lost in his own thoughts. Maybe she had really freaked him out for the last time. Maybe he had finally realized what kind of lunatic he was dealing with.

As they sat munching on their remaining doughnuts, the one thing that never happened, happened. Ed was silent.

I've made my share of sacrifices. In my line of work, nothing is more important than the job at hand—and everything else, *everything*, must be expendable. I've watched friends die. I've given up my identity. I've risked my life too many times to name. That's how it has had to be.

At one time, my feelings for my family fit into that mold. Undoubtedly, I loved them, but my work was the ultimate priority in our lives. I stoically accepted the months away from them, the stress it put on our lives, the danger it brought into our home. But that was when I had Katia. Looking back, I guess I never believed anything would actually happen to her.

But it did.

When I lost Katia—when *Gaia* and I lost Katia—I suddenly realized that there was something more important to me than doing the right thing for the world. That horrible night, I knew that I also wanted to do the right thing for my daughter. And the right thing for Gaia was for me to leave her. I still believe that.

So why do I stare at the phone at least once a day—agonizing over what it would be like just to hear her voice? Why do I write her letter after letter—knowing I can never mail them? Why do I keep coming up with a new, ridiculous plan to get back to New York and take her away with me?

And why, when I am halfway around the world on a mission that could save thousands of lives, do I only seem to care about one?

Out there
somewhere,
smelling
perfect and
looking like **still**
a goddess in **no**
faded cargo **call**
pants and a
rumpled
sweatshirt.

SAM MOON ROLLED OVER ONTO

Not Having Gaia

his back, kicked his flannel sheets away from his legs, and realized he was smiling. It felt *really* odd. He blinked open his eyes and looked around his room, confused in his half-asleep haze.

Sam never woke up smiling. He usually woke up gritting his teeth—something his dentist said was due to an excess amount of anxiety. Sam never felt stressed enough during his waking hours to grind down his teeth, but apparently the normally relaxing act of sleep made him tense up.

There was, however, a very good reason for this anomaly. And her name was Gaia Moore.

The grin widened just at the thought of her name. It grew almost painful when he remembered the kiss.

He couldn't believe he'd finally done it. Finally felt those perfect lips on his. She'd been so tentative. Careful. Almost as if she'd never been kissed before. But that wasn't possible. Not a girl like her. He only wished he might have stood out among the dozens of guys she'd probably had throwing themselves at her her entire life.

Stood out, that was, if she even happened to

remember the kiss at all. When she'd passed out in his arms due to severe head trauma, the chances of her recalling the most important moment of his entire life seemed pretty slim.

Sam ran a hand over his wavy, brownish red hair and squeezed his eyes shut. He'd called the hospital to find out if Gaia was okay on Friday, and they'd told him she'd been released that afternoon. So she was fine. Living. Breathing. Out there somewhere, smelling perfect and looking like a goddess in faded cargo pants and a rumpled sweatshirt.

But did she remember that he'd said he loved her? Did she even care?

Sam's stomach clenched, and he turned over onto his side. All he wanted to do was contact Gaia and make her answer his questions. And a moment later all he wanted to do was avoid her for the rest of his life so that he could save that one perfect kiss in his heart. So that he wouldn't be open to rejection. Ridicule. Laughter. From the one girl he'd ever loved.

It was, after all, very possible that she'd only kissed him back *because* of the severe head trauma. She'd probably thought she was kissing Joshua Jackson or something.

The self-deprecation train came to a grinding halt when a loud pounding sounded at Sam's dorm-room door. He sat up straight in bed, startled by the sudden noise.

"Yeah," Sam said.

The door flew open, and Keon Walters, Sam's physics lab partner, came storming into the room, his arms overflowing with books.

"What the—"

"Glad you got your beauty rest, Moon," Keon said, dropping the books on the floor with an ominous thud. "Did you forget the mandatory review session we had this morning?"

Sam's stomach dropped. "Uh, kind of," he said.

Keon hovered over the bed, his arms crossed over his nylon jacket as he eyed Sam with `barely veiled disdain`. "You better thank your lucky ass that you've got me for a partner," he said. "I told Krause your mother was at Mount Sinai with a colon thing. I laid it on so thick, I think he's sending flowers."

Sam rubbed his forehead, still trying to fully wake up. "Thanks, man," he said, eyeing the strewn books and papers lying next to his bed. They didn't look fun. "What is all that stuff?"

They both stared at the pile for a moment as apprehension seeped into Sam's veins. He had a bad feeling about this. Finally Keon sighed and lowered himself onto the end of Sam's bed. He took off his little round glasses and rubbed at his eyes. "That, my friend, would be required reading for the final."

"Please tell me you're kidding," Sam said. There

was no way he could absorb that much information on top of everything they'd already learned this semester. What was Krause thinking? He was an undergrad, not a Ph.D. candidate.

Keon leveled him with a glare. "Do I look like I'm kidding?" He crouched and started to neaten the load into two piles. "I figure if we split up the work and take notes, we *might* finish about five seconds before the exam."

Sam leaned back on his pillow, marveling at how one's outlook on life could shift so drastically in the space of about five minutes.

Gaia. Kiss. Love. Happiness.

Rejection. Loneliness. Regret. Misery.

Krause. Study. Death. Hell.

"Are you coming or what?" Keon said, picking up one of the stacks of books and raising his eyebrows at Sam. He was already halfway to the door.

"Where?" Sam asked, trying in vain to clear the soft Gaia images out of his head and replace them with velocity equations.

Keon clicked his tongue and rolled his eyes as if he were talking to a petulant five-year-old. "Library," he said, shifting his weight from one leg to the other. When Sam didn't move, Keon let out an exasperated breath. "Fine. If you're going to make me be the mommy here, I'll do it."

Sam rolled his eyes. "Keon—"

"Do you or do you not have to maintain a three-point-seven to keep your scholarship?" Keon interrupted. "Because if *I* had a full ride, and I had disappeared for two days before midterms and missed about ten classes for no apparent reason, I know I'd be scared shitless enough to handcuff myself to a reading-room cubicle."

Sam just blinked at Keon, a sudden pressure squeezing his chest. He hadn't missed those classes for no reason. He'd missed them for Gaia. And he'd disappeared before midterms because he was kidnapped, which also had something to do with Gaia, though he still didn't know what. Sam had been arrested for Gaia; he'd gotten his ass kicked for Gaia; he'd almost lost his girlfriend on several occasions.

He'd almost lost his life.

Sam dropped his head into his hands. God, he was pathetic. Physics was only the worst of a long list of problems. If he lost his scholarship, his future was toast. And for what? For a girl who might or might not know he loved her. Who might or might not care. This had to stop. Or at least be put on hold.

"Get your scrawny white ass out of bed and let's go," Keon said.

"Right behind you, man," Sam said, swinging his legs over the side of the bed. He eyed his designated workload and sighed. It wouldn't be *that* bad. And if he held off on seeing Gaia until it was all over, it would make the studying that much easier. It would give him a goal to work for. And some room to concentrate.

Right now he needed all the help he could get.

BY THE TIME THE DIGITAL CLOCK

next to her bed switched from 6:59 to 7:00, Heather Gannis had been staring at the red numbers for three

Distraction

hours and twenty-three minutes. Her eyes were dry. Her stomach was empty. But she didn't want to get out of bed. Getting out of bed meant facing her parents. Her sisters. The world in general, and she just wasn't up to it.

The past two days had been bad enough. Waiting for Sam to call. Trying to look like she wasn't waiting for Sam to call. Inconspicuously picking up the phone five times an hour just to make sure the damn thing was still working. It always was.

But now it was morning again. Two whole days had come and gone.

Still no call, even though he'd broken her heart.

And walked out on her.

And told her he was obsessed with Gaia Moore.

After everything she'd been through—everything she'd tolerated and fought against and forgiven—this could really be the end. Of SamandHeather. HeatherandSam.

The end of everything.

Heather squeezed her eyes shut, telling herself to get a grip. Self-pity wasn't something she entertained very often. Hardly ever, actually. But it was hard to avoid this time. It was the holidays. The one time of year she wasn't supposed to have to *pretend* to be happy. The one time of year when it usually came naturally. But not now. Thanks to Sam.

The only thing keeping her going was that the words had never been said. No one had said "I think we should break up," or "It's over." Sam hadn't out-and-out dumped her for Gaia. And even though she'd told him she didn't want to see him, it wasn't too late to take it back. *She* had kicked *him* out. She could take him back.

There was still hope.

There was a tentative knock at her door, but Heather ignored it, rolling onto her other side so that the clock wouldn't be able to mock her anymore. She wasn't going to move from this bed until she heard the phone ring. Or until Sam showed up at her door with flowers and possibly jewelry. Until he . . .

"No," Heather said to herself suddenly, finally sitting up and pulling her covers away from her body.

21

She wasn't going to wallow. She refused. Heather knew from experience that there was only one way to deal with a situation like this.

Distraction. Forced activity. She'd get dressed. Go out. See people. Maybe even buy something if she could scrounge up enough cash.

And sooner or later he would call. He had to.

He always did.

Eventually.

There was something very satisfying about hearing them scream. He usually let them get out one good, loud one before he covered their mouths. No one ever responded to one quick scream. They wrote it off as playing. Or a spider sighting. Or crying wolf.

And he so loved the scream.

It made him feel alive. It pumped him up.

It made the sex so much better.

He sat down on his floor and pulled out his black lock box from beneath his bed, flying through the combination with a quick three flicks of the wrist. Inside was his prized possession. The only thing he'd ever had worth locking up.

His journal. His list. His conquests.

He pulled out the tattered book with its dog-eared pages and cloth cover that was just starting to pull away from the

cardboard beneath. Soon it would
be time for a new book. But it
would be so hard to let this one
go. It was like an old friend. It
knew all his secrets. All his
successes. All his triumphs.

Turning to the first blank
page, he rolled the end of his
pen around inside his mouth,
carefully composing his opening.
This wasn't just a place to brag.
It was literature. One day, when
he was long gone, people would
read these pages and know him.
Know everything he was.

They would be awed.

He uncapped the pen and
started his entry.

Sunday, November 28th.
Thanksgiving holiday.
It certainly was a day for giv-
ing thanks. And Regina Farrell will
thank me one day. When she finally
admits to herself that she'll never
have anyone better . . .

Yes, she'd just committed herself to an actual social function.

gaia the brave

GAIA STOOD ON LINE IN THE CAFE-
teria on Monday afternoon
between two groups of
people who couldn't possibly have been more irritat-
ing. The FOHs—short
for Friends of Heather—
and the turtleneck-
wearing jock boys. If
there was ever a time to
cave in to modern tech-

Basic Get-Away-from-Me Signals

nology and use a Walkman, this was it. Words were
being wasted all around her, and she would have given
anything for a nice pair of headphones and a lot of
guitar-type noise.

"Omigod!" one FOH squealed. "You totally should
have been at CBGB's last night. The hottest guy
opened for Fearless. He was like a Lenny-Rob hybrid."

"Not possible," FOH number two said, sniffing a
bowl of Jell-O in a perfect imitation of a rabbit and re-
placing the bowl on the counter. "God couldn't possibly have blessed anyone with genes like that."

"He's playing again in two weeks," said FOH number three, the one with the biggest hair ever to spring
from a scalp. "Come and see for yourself."

"I am so there," FOH number two promised, placing her nearly empty tray in front of the register.
"*I* was at the Melody last night, and you . . ."

Foe number two trailed off as she glanced in Gaia's direction and noticed her not-staring. Her top lip actually curled up, and she huffed as she turned her back on Gaia, adjusting her tight leather jacket.

"Do you *see* what she's eating?" FOH number one sneered. All three FOHs turned to glare at Gaia's tray. Meatballs. Mashed-potato-like substance. Bowl of Jell-O not sniffed by FOH number two. Roll with tons of butter patties.

"Do you want some creamed corn, hon?" the lunch lady asked in a pleasant voice.

"Yeah," Gaia answered, mostly to disgust the FOHs. It worked. They all exchanged a very unoriginal look of grossed-outedness, paid for their food, and scurried away.

"There you go, hon," the big lady behind the counter said, heaping on the corn. She smiled at Gaia like she always did, and Gaia attempted smiling back. It didn't work, of course, but it was worth the try. Every student in this school might hate her, but at least she was universally loved by the lunch ladies. Gaia was pretty sure she was the only one who actually ate their food.

Gaia handed the woman at the register a crumpled ball of cash and automatically headed for the table she and Ed usually shared. Back corner, underneath the graph that broke down the four food groups. She was about to cut left when someone blocked her path.

This was so not the time for anyone to be starting up with her. Not on a Monday on which she'd woken up with a headache and the knowledge that Sam hadn't contacted her once all weekend.

Actually, maybe someone *should* start with her. She could use a scapegoat. "You're a brave girl," a slow, drawly voice said.

Gaia looked up into the deepest brown pair of eyes she'd ever seen. Spiky, messy hair. Sideburns. Expensive flannel. Not threatening. Definitely not asking for a beating.

"Are you going to move?" Gaia asked, shifting her tray slightly. Bad idea. Her plate of meatballs slid precariously close to the edge, taking everything with it. It was going over, and there was nothing she could do. More public spillage for the Spillage Queen.

"Careful," Sideburns said, righting the tray with lightning-quick reflexes. The kid in the chair next to them pulled himself a little closer to his table.

"Uh, thanks," Gaia told Sideburns. This was exactly the type of situation Gaia attempted to avoid at all costs. Was she supposed to try to converse with the guy, try to ignore him and look cool, try to . . . *flirt*? It was all too much for her socially impaired self to handle, so she attempted to move again. Unfortunately, he was still holding on to her tray.

"Aren't you going to ask me why I think you're so

brave?" he asked, ducking his chin in an attempt to make eye contact. What was this guy's deal? Was he immune to basic get-away-from-me signals?

"No," Gaia said. Exasperation. There. He had to get that.

He released her tray, crossing his arms over his rather broad chest but not moving out of the way. Gaia turned around to head back in the other direction, but a complicated melange of backpacks, chairs, and legs blocked her path. So much for the ignoring-and-looking-cool option.

When she turned around again, Sideburns was grinning. "It's just that in the three and a third years I've been here, I've never seen anyone eat Greta's meatballs."

Oh, how very original. "There's a first time for everything," Gaia said. She took a step toward him, hoping he wasn't going to force her to take him down with a quick flick of her foot to his shin. He seemed harmless enough, but if she didn't eat soon, this Monday was going to go from suckfest to hell pit in a matter of seconds.

"Okay, okay." Sideburns relented, turning sideways to let her pass. But as he did he flicked a little pink piece of paper out of his pocket and dropped it on Gaia's tray. It had black writing on it, and the only word she could make out without actually appearing to be interested was *music*.

"Having a little party tonight," he said, holding up his hands to give her more room. "You should show."

The irrational part of Gaia's brain couldn't believe that someone had just asked her to a party. Her. Public enemy number one. Other than Ed and Mary, no one had asked her to do anything at all since she'd arrived in New York. Except die, of course. The rational part of her brain formulated a sentence and sent it to her voice box.

"I'd rather sing 'Copacabana' in front of the entire school," she said, moving past him.

Sideburns laughed. "I'll rent a karaoke machine!" he called after her.

Gaia never smiled on Mondays. But if she did, the exchange might have been worthy of one.

AS GAIA LOWERED HERSELF INTO

the chair across from Ed, he plucked a little piece of bright pink paper from her overloaded tray.

Screw Him

"'Come one. Come all,'" Ed read aloud. "'Free beer. Free music. Free love.'" He chuckled and placed the tiny flyer on the table between them. "Going hippie on me, Gaia?"

She lifted one shoulder as she took a swig of her soda. "Some guy gave it to me," she said, jabbing a meatball with her fork. Ed's stomach turned over, and not just because she was actually consuming a cafeteria-made meat substance.

Another guy?

More guys?

Didn't he have enough to deal with?

"Who?" Ed asked, trying to keep the psychotic jealousy out of his voice. It was still there, but if she noticed, she didn't show a sign. She just chomped on another meatball as her eyes scanned the room.

"Him," she said finally, pointing with her fork across the large cafeteria at Tim Racenello. Abercrombie & Fitch boy. Skier. Former friend. Definitely charming. Damn.

"Are you going to go?" Ed asked, pushing his chicken noodle soup sans chicken—a cafeteria specialty—around with his spoon. *Please say you're not going to go. Please say you're not going to go.*

"Ed. Come on. No," she said.

Cool.

"I was kind of thinking about going to see Sam tonight," she said, actually sounding tentative. "You know, find out . . . if there's anything to find out."

Not cool.

"Well, I'll go if you'll go," Ed offered, putting down his spoon and laying his hands flat on the table. The

31

action helped to keep him from sinking into the bottomless black pit that had opened beneath his chair at the sound of Sam's name. Amazing. It was just one little syllable. Sam. More like a grunt than a name.

Yet it held so much power.

"Go where?" Gaia asked, confused. Ed felt his delirious mind step off its rambling path and snap into the now. He wondered if she thought he was offering to go to Sam's with her. Not likely.

"The party," Ed said, forcing a smirk. "Focus, G."

Gaia froze with a forkful of mashed potatoes halfway into her mouth. It took her a couple of seconds to decide whether to eat or talk. She did both.

"You want to go to this thing," she said as soon as she'd swallowed. Statement. Disbelieving statement. When had he lost the moniker of Ed "Shred" Fargo, party animal? As if he really had to ask that question.

"Tim's pretty cool," Ed told her, hoping against hope she would go against every fiber of her being and agree to go with him. "We used to hang out before my hanging involved the chair."

Gaia's gaze flicked in Tim's direction. "He stopped hanging out with you after . . ." She let the sentence trail off, probably because she still didn't know how Ed had ended up without leg power.

"No," Ed answered the unfinished question. "I

stopped hanging out with him. I stopped hanging out with a lot of people." He immediately felt his spirits start to wane. He was coming dangerously close to losing the nonchalant thing he'd gone to great lengths to develop. Clearing his throat, Ed pushed all melancholy thoughts aside. He'd rejoined the social world a long time ago. There was no need to dwell on the dark past. The now demanded his full attention.

"So are you going to go with me or not?" Ed asked, downing a spoonful of his now cold soup. Somehow it tasted better cold. Took the edge off.

"I don't know, Ed. . . ."

She was thinking of Sam. He knew it. He could tell by the regretful little cloud in her eyes. Like she was thinking of him and ashamed of herself for thinking of him. There was only one way to make Gaia agree to party with him. The one way he could get Gaia to do almost anything. Get her angry. Or at least righteously indignant.

"Sam hasn't called, has he?" Ed asked, feeling like the soap scum wad in the corner of his shower. The one with the black mildew gathering on it.

Her eyes flashed. Score one for the soap scum. "No," she said flatly.

"Then why are you planning on going over there?" Ed asked casually, pushing his tray away. It hit Gaia's and moved it an inch over the lip of the table toward her.

"I'm not," she said, pushing her own tray back. Ed's went two and a half inches off the end. At least.

"Then go to the party," Ed said, pushing their trays back so that they were centered evenly on the table. He laced his fingers together and rested his elbows on the arms of his wheelchair. "Screw him."

Gaia blinked. Ed could practically see the little consonants and vowels that made up his words sinking into her brain.

"Fine," she said. "Let's go."

HE WAS IN HER ENGLISH CLASS. HOW

convenient. She'd never noticed him before, but there he was. Front row, window seat. Good view and a fast escape route. And he was eating a Hostess cupcake. That was comforting. At least he had good taste in food.

Gaia made her way across the room, her battered sneakers

First Ever Monday Smile

squeaking loudly on the linoleum floor. He didn't see her, and she didn't exactly have an opening line, so she dropped her bag on his desk with a half flop, half clatter.

34

If he was startled, he hid it well. He chewed, swallowed, and looked up. His eyebrows arched when he saw her, but he recovered quickly and leaned back in his chair, smiling up at her. He had chocolate stuck to his two front teeth.

"If it isn't Gaia the Brave," he said, running his tongue quickly along his bottom teeth to clear the sugary goo. It didn't help the top part of his mouth, but Gaia wasn't about to point that out.

"Got another one?" she asked, pushing a strand of hair behind her ear. It fell right back into place, and she didn't touch it. Pointless. As were all attempts at grooming in Gaia's book.

Sideburns Tim experienced momentary confusion marked by a quick squint. "Another what?"

"Cupcake," Gaia said, shifting her feet. That was when she noticed that Heather Gannis was sitting two rows behind Sideburns Tim, shooting Gaia a glare that was now so familiar to her, Gaia could probably have mimicked it in her sleep. She looked Heather directly in the eye and spoke to Tim. "If you give me a cupcake, I'll come to your little party."

Heather visibly paled. Even her normally lined lips were white. It was all Gaia could do to keep from breaking the no-smiling-on-Mondays rule. It was an odd Monday when that almost happened twice.

Sideburns Tim pulled a single wrapped cupcake out of his bag and tossed it at Gaia. She caught it in one hand without even blinking.

"I don't know if it's your lucky day or mine," he said with a smirk that displayed a small dimple just behind a very light layer of stubble. Probably sexy in some circles. In Heather's circle, from the look of pure horror on the girl's face.

"It's yours," Gaia said. His smirk deepened. She pocketed her cupcake and walked to the back of the room, allowing herself a brief moment of pride. It had been a long time since she'd come out with a comeback line she liked on the spot and not approximately three and a half hours later, when it was useless.

The fury was coming off Heather in waves. As Gaia took her seat, she wondered if Heather had spoken to Sam this weekend—if she knew what had happened between Gaia and her beloved boyfriend. If she did know, Gaia really wished the girl would clue her in. But somehow Gaia doubted that was going to happen.

In fact, since she hadn't received any idle death threats, Gaia figured Heather was thus far clueless. Maybe even more clueless than Gaia was. Gaia at least knew she'd been in Sam's room. Worn Sam's clothes. Even if there had been no touching of the lips, she was sure Heather would throw a Springer-worthy psycho tantrum if she knew what Gaia knew.

Leaning back in her chair, Gaia tore open the packaging on her cupcake and propped her knees up on the desk in front of her. Sure, Sam hadn't called. Yes, she'd just committed herself to an actual social function. And yes, she was living with a heinous woman who wore slutty clothes and bad perfume.

But the thought that she actually knew something about Sam that Heather didn't was the thing that brought the first ever full-on Monday smile to Gaia Moore's lips.

HEATHER GANNIS WAS HAVING A

Sick of Everything

very bad day, and trying to keep herself from screaming in the middle of English class wasn't making it any easier. Her boyfriend was avoiding her, her best friends had all gone out the night before without her and couldn't stop talking about it, and the only reason she hadn't gone was because she had fully expected said boyfriend to call her, which he, of course, hadn't.

What if he'd spent the weekend with Gaia? What if he'd left Heather's apartment and gone directly to wherever the reject holed herself up? After all this time and everything they'd been through, had Gaia finally won?

Heather traced the pink line down the side of her paper with her pen, pushing so hard, she tore a hole in the page. She was getting so sick of everything. Sick of Sam's avoidance-of-conflict policy. Sick of feeling unsure. Sick of friends who dropped money on cab rides and bars like they were a necessity. Sick, most of all, of Gaia Moore.

Mr. MacGregor sauntered into the room and immediately started passing out pop quiz papers. Lovely. What kind of person gave a quiz the day after Thanksgiving weekend? It was like the man lived to see students suffer. What next? Was her hair going to start falling out in clumps?

Heather adjusted the collar on her itchy wool sweater and pushed her thick brown mane back behind her shoulders. Whatever she did, she couldn't let her misery show. She needed to constantly keep the three Cs in high gear. Cool, calm, collected. Otherwise there would be questions from her legion of followers. And questions, at this point, were something she couldn't handle.

Missy Ryan handed the quiz papers back, and Heather took one and passed the stack along. Nothing on the page looked remotely familiar. Her body temperature skyrocketed. Heather turned the paper over with a slap and took a long breath. She had to chill. Now.

She hazarded a glance over her shoulder at Gaia.

She, of course, was busily scratching away at her paper, oblivious to the world around her. The girl practically looked happy. That never happened. Something in the cosmic balance of Heather's universe had shifted, and she didn't like it.

Tim asking Gaia to tonight's party was the last straw. Heather faced forward again and twisted a lock of hair around her finger violently, yanking at her scalp. The only thing that had kept Heather going this weekend was looking forward to tonight's little shindig. She'd talked it up to all her friends, making sure they would all be there. There was nothing better than a free party with free dancing and free alcohol, even when her boyfriend was freakishly AWOL.

But a party with Gaia Moore was another story.

A party with Gaia Moore was something to avoid at all costs.

From: smoon@alloymail.com
To: gaia13@alloymail.com
Time: 2:45 P.M.
Re: Thanksgiving
    Gaia,
    I still can't believe you were actually here.
I can't stop thinking about you and when I'm
going to see you again. I just
                <<DELETE>>

From: smoon@alloymail.com
To: gaia13@alloymail.com
Time: 2:46 P.M.
Re: Thanksgiving

Gaia,

   I hope you're okay. The doctors said you would
be, but I hated to leave you, anyway. I haven't
written before because—

<<DELETE>>

From: smoon@alloymail.com
To: gaia13@alloymail.com
Time: 2:47 P.M.
Re: Thanksgiving

Gaia,

   Do you even remember what happened between us?
I remember every detail. Every smell. Every
touch. Everything. If you don't remember . . .
I'll probably die, actually.

<<DELETE>>

From: smoon@alloymail.com
To: gaia13@alloymail.com
Time: 2:48 P.M.
Re: Thanksgiving

Gaia,

Thanks for an . . . interesting Thanksgiving.
I'll never forget it. I want to see you, but I
have finals right now and I really have to concentrate on that. Can I call you when I'm done?

—Sam

<<SEND>>

GAIA REALLY WANTED A DOG. AS

Kibble she stood outside the fence that sur-
rounded the dog run in Washington
Square Park, watching the little
pink tongues and the little
padded feet and the little twitching
noses, she wanted nothing else more.

Imagine having something in your life that lived
for nothing but you. Imagine unconditional love.
Imagine a friend that could hide no secrets. A friend
that couldn't hurt you, who would protect you at all
costs, and all you had to do was throw him some kibble every once in a while. A friend who, yeah, smelled
bad but hung out by the door every day just to see
your face.

Gaia grinned. She could have just described Ed Fargo.

She gripped the fence with her frozen hands and watched a scruffy little mutt with a black body and brown ears chase a squirrel out through a hole in the other side of the fence.

Of course if she did get a dog, she'd probably figure out how to drive it away. She seemed to be very skilled at that. But maybe, just maybe, she only repelled humans.

With a huge sigh Gaia leaned back her head and watched the steam of her breath dance up into the air. After ten minutes of doing the go-in-don't-go-in boogie in front of Sam's dorm, she felt good to be momentarily still in the presence of the frenzied mayhem in front of her. For once she felt like the one sane being in a twenty-yard radius. Funny how she had to be in the company of a bunch of ankle-biting, loudly yelping animals that sniffed each other's butts in order to feel normal.

"Sadie! Sadie! Over here!" someone called, causing a little collie to look up from its dirt inhaling.

"Crystal!"

"Katie!"

"Buffy!"

"Aaaahhh! Get it off me! Get it off me!"

"Katie! Katie, no! Bad dog!"

Gaia smirked as she found Katie at the far side of the run, outside the fence. She was a beautiful golden retriever who had latched onto some suit's shoelace and was pulling back, her four feet planted firmly on the ground.

"Katie!"

"Gaia!"

"Katie! Stop it now!"

"Gaia?"

"*Gaia?*"

A hand landed on her shoulder, and Gaia spun around so fast, her hair whipped into her eyes and temporarily blinded her. She brought her hands to her face and shoved the hair away.

"Hey," a familiar voice said. "This is some exciting after-school entertainment."

Mary. Gaia felt a little stirring in her stomach at the memory of her last encounter with Mary Moss. And everything that had come after it. The cocaine, followed up by the cold, the beating, the theft, the explosion, the blood, and then all the stuff she couldn't quite remember.

"I can see how it doesn't live up to *your* standards of excitement," Gaia replied. She wanted to take back the words a moment later when she saw the hurt flash through Mary's eyes, but she didn't. Gaia was bad at relationships and even worse at apologies. She turned back to the dogs and focused on a patch of ground in front of her.

Mary stepped up beside her, shoving her hands in the pockets of her long wool coat. "Guess I deserved that," she said tentatively, seeming to stare at the same spot of dirt as if it could reveal Gaia's thoughts. "Did you get my letter?"

"Yeah," Gaia said. The letter had explained how Mary had a serious problem. How she wanted to get clean. How she wanted to get clean for Gaia. And Gaia was happy for Mary. She really was. But the whole doing-it-for-Gaia was just a little too much pressure, even if it was accompanied by a lot of chocolate. "I got it," she said finally.

"And?" Mary asked. She reached out and laced her pink-gloved fingers through the fence. Her fingers looked very small and very thin. Gaia looked into Mary's questioning, vulnerable eyes.

"And . . . I think it's . . . good that you want to, you know, quit," Gaia said. Damn, she was articulate. But she didn't know what she was supposed to do or say. And it seemed like one of those situations that called for exactly the right thing. Gaia was pretty sure she'd never said exactly the right thing in her life.

Mary took a deep breath, shifting her feet so that the gravel and silt crunched beneath her boots. "Well, I'm looking into some stuff, like NA and . . . stuff," she said, stumbling over her own words. "My parents are helping. I, uh . . . I told them everything. I figure I can't do this without them, and besides completely freaking out and crying and the whole deal, they're actually being really cool. But I need your help with a very important step in the clean-Mary plan."

"What's that?" Gaia asked. She noticed for the first time that her friend's pale skin was paler than normal, her unruly red hair oddly flat. The girl needed that unconditional love Gaia was longing for moments ago. She needed it maybe more than Gaia did.

"The good, clean fun part," Mary said with a smile that held just a trace of the Mary-mischief Gaia had learned to love.

"Good, clean fun, huh?" Gaia said with a smirk. Little did poor Mary know that Gaia wasn't exactly an expert on the subject of fun. She wasn't even a novice. Up until she met Mary, she'd been pretty sure she was, in fact, immune to fun. Still, she couldn't exactly let Mary down. It was time to throw the girl some kibble.

"I think I can handle that," Gaia said, pulling her jacket closer to her body and shivering slightly as a breeze fought its way past her collar and down her back. She looked Mary directly in the eye. "I just have one question," she said, causing the smile to disappear from Mary's face. "How do I know you're telling the truth? That you really want to do this."

Mary gripped the fence harder, and her face became pale. For a moment Gaia thought her friend might faint, but she held her own. Seconds later, her features softened and a little color returned to her cheeks.

"Because," she said, her voice just slightly shaky. She cleared her throat and tossed back her hair. "Because I'm going to stay here with you and watch these stupid dogs." Mary's brow wrinkled slightly as she glanced around at the assembled owners with their steaming coffees and their leashes wrapped around their hands and wrists. "And you are going to explain to me what, exactly, is supposed to be interesting about this."

Okay, so maybe the girl was sincere. Gaia tilted her head toward the fence, inviting Mary to come closer. When their foreheads were practically touching the cold metal, Gaia brought her tingling cheek close to Mary's in conspiratorial spy fashion.

"See that dog right there?" Gaia asked, pointing out Katie, who was now terrorizing Sadie the collie by barking at her and chasing her every time she sat down. Mary nodded and smiled. "Keep an eye on that one," Gaia said. "I think you'll like her."

"Come on, Gaia," Ella said, placing her napkin on the table. She was all glee. "Tell George about your little Sam."

ready and willing

THE LIBRARY WAS PRETTY. THE books? Gorgeous. The leather chair felt like a little piece of cloud. But the people were all very uninteresting. Bland. Ugly, even.

None of them were Gaia Moore.

Sam was fully aware that at least three students in the East Asian Library were staring at him with a disturbed sort of curiosity. Why shouldn't they be? He was kicked back in a big green chair, his feet up on the table in front of him, about ten large textbooks piled around him—and he was smiling like an idiot. Like he was lying on a massage table on a white beach in the Caribbean.

It was almost finals week, and Sam Moon was summer-vacation giddy.

"What are you on, man?" whispered Sam's suite mate, Mike Suarez, leaning across the table. "And can I have some?"

"Shhh!" Keon refused to let anyone get out a sentence without scolding them. Sam and Mike both glanced at him, then smirked.

"Nope. Definitely not. None for you," Sam said, adjusting the physics book on his lap. Out of the corner of his eye he saw Keon shake his head in frustration, but the kid was just going to have to deal. Sam couldn't render himself mute for two weeks' worth of studying and exam taking.

Mike's whole forehead scrunched up, and he looked like he was suddenly reconsidering their living arrangements. "Well, at least cut the smiley face act. You're freaking people out, and we can't be driven from East Asia."

"Right," Sam said, attempting to force down the corners of his mouth. "No problem." For a split second he tried to concentrate on his book, but then he found himself looking around the room, Gaia thoughts flitting in and out of his mind. The East Asian room was the most comfortable, quiet study nook in the library, but only a select few people knew about it. Mike had found out about the cozy chairs and relatively private tables from one of his frat brothers and had let Sam and Keon in on the secret. Today they'd shown up early enough to stake a claim in the prime corner, right at the end of the stacks.

Sam had promised Keon he was ready to cram. Get down to business. Study like it was going out of style.

But he couldn't stop thinking about Gaia.

He could still feel her hands on his shoulders. Her tongue grazing his lips. Her—

"Is it Heather?" Mike whispered, causing Sam's little fantasy world to disappear in a poof of guilt-tinged smoke.

"Is what Heather?" Sam asked, glancing over his shoulder. Had she found him at the NYU library? Had she tracked him down? Somehow Sam wouldn't have been surprised to see her sauntering through the room, ready to grab his arm and force an in-depth analysis of the big blowout.

"The I-just-got-me-some look on your face," Mike said with a grin.

"Shhhhhh!" Keon exploded.

"Give me a break," Mike hissed. He looked back at Sam. "Did you and Heather get busy last night or what?"

Sam sighed in relief and righted himself in his chair. *Getting busy* wasn't exactly the phrase he would have used to describe what had gone on between him and Heather over Thanksgiving. Before he'd walked out on her. Before he'd gone back to his dorm. Before he'd found Gaia there. Waiting for him.

"Not exactly," he said, pushing himself back in his seat.

"Then what is it, Moon?" Mike asked, his brown eyes twinkling. "Some other girl?"

Sam cleared his throat. "I thought we were studying," he said, highlighting a random sentence on the glossy page of his physics text. He could feel that Mike was still staring at him, so he kept pretending to read until the kid gave up and flopped back in his chair, the cushions letting out a little hissing sound as air escaped through the seams.

Swallowing hard, Sam forced his eyes to the top of the page and started to read for real. The mention of Heather had brought him back down to earth, hard.

Yes, they'd fought. She'd told him to leave. But he knew Heather, and he knew she said a lot of things she didn't mean. Which meant that she was still technically his girlfriend. Which meant that Thanksgiving night in his dorm, he'd cheated on her. With the one person she hated more than anyone else on the planet.

Sam had no clue what to do about Heather. He had even less of a clue how to proceed with Gaia. She wasn't a normal ask-her-out-on-a-date-and-don't-forget-to-bring-flowers type of girl. That had been proven many times over since the first time he'd met her.

With a deep breath, Sam pushed Heather and Gaia out of his mind and picked up his notebook, flipping it open to the first page of notes.

Suddenly he was glad to have something as important and all consuming as finals to command his attention.

ONE LITTLE E-MAIL MESSAGE WAS

Ella's Salvation

all it took.

Even after Heather. Even after Marco. After David. After her father. After every deranged, psychotic, evil, slimy, grime-covered, bad-cologne-wearing midnight assailant. Even after dealing with each and every one of these hateful beings, Gaia could quite honestly say she had never felt so much rage before in her life.

And from the look on Ella Niven's face, the woman was just smart enough to know that this rage was directed at her.

"You lied to me," Gaia said. There was no surprise in her voice. Only the rage. Ella's face went white for a moment underneath her layers of foundation and powder. She backed away from the foul-smelling sludge she was frying on the stove and crossed her arms over her chest. Gaia wondered if Ella was remembering when Gaia punched her. Remembering and fearing.

God, she hoped she was.

"I don't appreciate your tone, Gaia," she said, wiping her hands on her ruffled apron.

"I was with someone on Thanksgiving," Gaia said, trying desperately to ignore the burning, acrid stench that was assailing her nostrils and choking her airways. Her eyes were watering, and she suddenly registered the fact that Ella was actually cooking—or attempting an unreasonable facsimile thereof. She never cooked. Was the woman actually trying to kill her?

Ella took a deep breath—how she managed it, Gaia

had no idea—and smoothed her blazing red hair back from her face. "And how, exactly, does that make me a liar?"

"You told me there was no one there, at the hospital," Gaia said, leaning onto the counter in front of her, her veins throbbing in her forehead. Ella had hated Gaia from the moment she'd first walked through the door. Gaia had picked up on it immediately and hated the woman right back. But why did Ella feel the need to take every single thing away from her? Gaia had never even met her before she came to Perry Street, but the woman was brimming with malice. Why?

Ella's amphibian green eyes narrowed into angry slits. "That's right," she said calmly. "There was no one with you at the hospital. God only knows what you did before then. I did tell you they found you outside some dorm, babbling about someone named Sam." She ran her fingernail along the side of her mouth, like a cat who'd just finished off the forbidden goldfish. "Is that who you're talking about?" she said with a light laugh. "Maybe he'd just kicked you out of his room."

There was a moment without air. No intake whatsoever. A moment when Gaia's heart felt like it was about to burst open from the pressure.

Her first inclination was to launch herself at Ella and make her take it back.

Her second inclination was to entertain the idea that the woman might be right.

That was the standard Gaia-as-masochist inclination.

But no. It wasn't possible. Sam's e-mail had said thanks. He'd said he wanted to see her again. She was no relationship expert, but if he'd booted her, he wouldn't be saying that. Right?

And he wouldn't have left her outside in the cold, bruised and woozy and half comatose.

Not Sam.

Gaia rounded the counter and, in one long stride, got within centimeters of Ella's pointy little face. She was quite satisfied when Ella flinched.

"I swear to you, Ella, if you don't tell me the truth right now—"

There was a door slam, and two pairs of eyes darted to the kitchen entry.

"George," Ella whispered, sounding like she was uttering the name of salvation.

"I'm home!" George shouted from the foyer. "What smells so interesting?"

Gaia felt her muscles untighten, and she pulled away reluctantly. The threats were going to have to wait for another day unless she wanted to explain to George why she'd kicked his wife's skinny ass as his homecoming present.

Heart-to-Heart à la George

"AS SOON AS YOU'RE ALL WASHED up, come back down for dinner!" Ella called cheerily as Gaia slammed her way out of the kitchen and into the hallway, the heinous smell still clinging to her skin. George was shaking out his coat and hanging it up in the closet by the door. Gaia paused. He looked tired. Almost older.

"Hi, George," she said, going for the closet before he had a chance to close it. She pulled out her flimsy jacket and started to put it on, hoping he was so tired and jet-lagged, he wouldn't feel like starting up a conversation. She could talk to him about his trip later. She had to get out of this house, pronto.

Out of the corner of her eye she saw George's already wrinkled brow crease even deeper with concern. Damn. So close.

"Where are you going?" he asked, eyeing the arm that was half in, half out of the sleeve. "Aren't we about to eat? Ella told me this morning that she was going to give cooking a whirl."

He inhaled, and Gaia was gratified to see the tears spring to his eyes, not that he'd ever acknowledge them. "She was very excited," he said evenly.

"I'm not really hungry," Gaia said. She had been

55

starving, but the stench, Sam's e-mail, and the almost fight took that right out of her.

George sighed and shook his head slowly. His eyes looked all heavy and apprehensive, like he was a doctor about to tell a couple he'd done everything he could, but he just couldn't save their kid.

"Gaia, Ella told me all about what happened while I was away. I know things are hard for you right now—"

The squirming started immediately. Exactly how much had Ella told the poor old guy? Gaia wasn't certain how much his creaky little ticker could take. And she'd hate to be a cause of stress to George. Any more than she already was, anyway.

"With your father gone and your mother . . ."

Gaia's eyes focused on a tiny spiderweb in the corner behind George's head. Heart-to-hearts weren't her thing.

"And after this whole Christmas . . . I mean—" He brought a hand to his forehead and laughed at himself. "Thanksgiving mess . . ."

Apparently George wasn't very good at them, either.

"Well, I just want you to know that if there's anything you ever need to talk about . . . whether it's boys—"

"Stop." The word was out of Gaia's mouth like a

shot. George's face went from pink to crimson, and Gaia immediately felt guilty. "Sorry." She pulled on the hem of her baggy black sweater resolutely, inhaled, held back a choking cough, and looked him in the eye.

"Let's eat."

THERE WAS A WHITE BLOB, A

athetically
Unsordid

reddish brown blob, and a pile of what looked like dried sticks. Gaia gulped her water as Ella related the fascinating details of her day of beauty at Aveda. George kept nodding as if he knew exactly what his wife was talking about, but Gaia wasn't even sure what exfoliaters and sloughing cream were—which just reminded her what a pathetic excuse for a female she was. This had to be over soon.

"So, Gaia," Ella said, spooning a heap of the white mush into her mouth as she finished a harrowing tale of an acid peel gone awry—a story that suddenly made Gaia feel *glad* she was a pathetic excuse for a female. Ella licked her lips daintily and touched a napkin to her mouth. She did this after every single bite she took. It was starting to drive Gaia insane.

"What?" Gaia said tersely.

"I don't suppose you would want to tell us how *your* day went, would you?" Ella asked, shooting George a look as if seeking affirmation that she'd now officially done her duty. She'd acted interested.

"Not really," Gaia answered, pushing at her pile of sticks with her fork. A few toppled over the rim of her plate onto the white linen tablecloth. Ella glared at them, but Gaia didn't make a move to clean it up. Fewer sticks for her stomach.

George shifted in his seat slightly, gearing up to talk. Gaia silently prayed he wouldn't bring up the whole boy topic again.

"Are you making friends at that school yet?" he asked, bravely taking a bite from the reddish brown blob. The flinch was almost indiscernible.

"Oh, she's making friends," Ella said, her eyes on her food as a little satisfied smile played about her lips. "Just not at that school."

Gaia felt an angry blush color her cheeks, and she shot Ella a glare that should have turned her to vapor. In a perfect world. In this world, Ella just smirked back at her.

"Really?" George looked intrigued. Gaia shrugged. Like she was really going to share. There was nothing *to* share. Not yet. At least not with these people. Ella, after all, still quite possibly knew more than she did, a thought that did nothing for her already squirming stomach.

"Come on, Gaia," Ella said, placing her napkin on the table. She was all glee. "Tell George about your little Sam." The way she said the last three words made Gaia come unconscionably close to lifting her end of the table so that the entire meal slid into Ella's lap.

George smiled and looked from Ella to Gaia. The guy was definitely ready and willing. To hear what? That she might or might not have kissed the boyfriend of a girl she hated who also happened to be the most popular girl in school? That was sure to make George beam with pride. Not that Gaia cared.

"I have to go," Gaia said, standing up and letting her napkin slide from her lap onto the floor.

Ella's freshly waxed eyebrows arched. Gaia wondered if they colored those during her day of beauty, too, along with her fake red hair. "Don't tell me you have somewhere to be."

"Ella," George said in a tone that came close to a warning. Apparently he'd finally picked up on her ever sarcastic tone.

Gaia looked into Ella's eyes and paused. There wasn't just surprise and mockery there. There was something else. A guarded, defensive kind of look. Jealousy? Was that even possible?

"Party," she said, just to gauge the reaction. Ella blinked, and her expression went flat. Then she quickly looked away and picked up her water glass with one hand while fiddling with the gold pendant that always hung in her cleavage with the other. It *was* jealousy. Interesting.

"On a Monday?" George said. He looked at Ella as if he wasn't sure whether or not this was acceptable. Like Ella knew anything about propriety. Unfortunately, Ella was too preoccupied trying to look unfazed, and she didn't notice her own husband's stare for help. Gaia decided to put him out of his misery, if only so she could get out of here and put herself out of her own.

"I won't be late, George," she said, forcing a tight, hopefully reassuring, but probably just disturbing smile. She hoped he would just hurry up and tell her it was all right. If he didn't, she would sneak through the window, anyway, but it was much less trouble to go out through the front door.

"Okay," he said. "But you be careful out there. You never know—"

But Gaia was already down the hall and halfway up the steps to the relative privacy of her own room.

ONE PAIR OF CORDUROYS

What Ed Tried On

One pair of jeans
Two flannels
One V-necked shirt
A Hawaiian print button-down
Two baseball caps
One fisherman's cap
A pair of sunglasses
Two pairs of sneakers
One pair of in-line skates (for kicks)
Three T-shirts
One pocket watch
One fedora

THREE PAIRS OF JEANS

What Heather Tried On

Five of her sister's skirts
One skirt of her own
Three pairs of earrings
Her mother's pearls
One headband
Two barrettes
Three colors of lipstick, all in the brown family
One pair of ribbed tights
Four pairs of shoes—one clunky, one practical, two deadly

Two belts
Five blouses
One sweater
Two perfumes
Five bags
One choker

ONE T-SHIRT

One hooded sweatshirt
One pair of cargo pants
One pair of sneakers
One blue sock
One black sock
One piece of Bubble Yum

What Gaia Tried On

HEATHER GANNIS WAS NOT A STALKER.

Show Time

She might have looked like one, hanging out in the shadows on the corner of Fifth Avenue and Tenth Street—across the street from Sam's dorm—intently staring past the traffic on Tenth to keep a constant watch on the door. But she definitely was not a stalker. She was a girl with a boyfriend who was ignoring her. And that merited certain covert action.

Okay, certain stalkerish covert action.

Heather rubbed her gloved hands together and cupped them in front of her mouth, blowing into her palms. Her toes were tingly in her sexy-yet-unprotective shoes, and goose bumps were fighting their way to existence even under her thick wool coat.

Where was he? Sam was generally a nice guy. Couldn't he cut a nonstalker some slack?

The glass door of the dorm swung open just as a stiff wind blew directly into Heather's eyes, stinging them painfully and blurring her vision. There was a tall person-blob making his way down Fifth toward her, bending into the wind with his books tucked under his arm. It had to be him. Heather couldn't see his face clearly, but she could feel it in her gut. And the butterflies surrounding her heart started to do a nervous little dance.

It was show time.

She tossed her hair from her shoulders. Pressed her lips together. Straightened her posture. And started to search through her purse.

He had to see her first. That was key in the whole nonstalker plan.

Searching. Searching. He was coming across Tenth now. Searching. But there wasn't much more to search through. He was walking. Walking. He was right there. Her heart started to pound, and the search for nothing became more frantic. He was . . . He was . . . He was passing her by.

What?

"Sam?"

He stopped and turned around slowly, his whole body rigid. His face registered surprise, but the rest of him was pure discomfort.

Good.

"Heather," he said. He was probably expecting another fight. Or at least a reprimand for not having returned her e-mails and phone calls. He was in for a surprise.

"Hi!" she said brightly, walking up to him and giving him a quick kiss on the cheek. His stubbly face was still warm from inside, and as mad as she was at him, part of her just wanted to cuddle into him and not let go. Instead she pulled away quickly, pleased that he looked shocked. "Where are you going?" she asked.

It took him a moment to realize it was his turn to speak. "Library," he said. His gaze flicked over her outfit, and it was all Heather could do to keep from grinning. Now he would ask her where *she* was going, and she could say—

"I'd better get going," he said.

Wait. That wasn't his line.

"Uh . . ."

And that definitely wasn't hers.

Sam's face creased with regret, and he shoved his free hand into his pocket. "Listen," he said, backing away slightly. "I know we have to talk, but finals are next week, and I just got slammed with all this work—"

"I'm going to a party," Heather heard herself say. At least she thought it was her who had spoken. Her voice had come out sounding more like a plastic doll's with a voice box and a string.

"Good," Sam said. He couldn't care less.

What was going on here? When had she lost control of the situation? And why did it suddenly seem like all of the bundled-up passersby on the sidewalk were mocking her? Laughing at her. Telling her to wake up and see that it was all over.

Sam was on the move again. Backing away to freedom. "Well, I really have to . . ."

And then Heather was struck with an idea. She knew how to get his attention. And maybe hurt him the way he'd already obliviously hurt her.

"Everyone's going to be there," she said nonchalantly. "Tim, Megan, Ed, Gaia."

He stopped, and Heather's heart tore free from the veins and arteries that kept it alive. She hadn't counted on more hurt for her.

"Gaia?" he said.

Somehow Heather smiled a beautiful, perfect smile. "Yeah!" she said, now backing away herself. "Tim Racenello invited her. You should have seen how psyched she was. I don't know, but I think there may be something there. You know?" She tucked her hair behind her ear and continued to beam as if she were talking about her best friend finding true love. "Well, have fun studying."

As if he was going to get any work done now. He was going to sit in the library, obsessing about this. Heather could tell by the stricken look on his face. Unreal. He didn't even try to hide it.

She turned and plunged onto Fifth Avenue without even looking up at the traffic light. Part of her truly hoped a nice downtown bus would come along and flatten her. It wasn't like it could do her much more damage.

From: gaia13@alloymail.com
To: maryubuggin@alloymail.com
Time: 8:07 P.M.
Re: tonight

Mary—

Forgot to tell you Ed talked me into going to this party tonight. When you stop laughing, you should stop by. It's at 34th and 1st. Some big building with fountains in the lobby.

Show up and keep me company. I'm sure there will be plenty of mock-worthy people. Good, clean fun.

—Gaia

Normally, I don't go in with a plan. I never know who I'm going to want until I'm in the moment. I do have a special place in my heart for brunettes, though. They often think they're ordinary. Plain. Not-sexy. They act like they have something to prove. And that always makes things more interesting.

But I'm not averse to the occasional blond. Redhead. Asian, African American, Indian, Latina, etc., etc. I'm not averse to anything. Like I said, it depends on how I feel in the moment.

Tonight, however, I have a plan. Two, actually. One brunette. One blond. Maybe neither will resist. But hopefully at least one of them will.

It's the breaking-down process that makes for riveting reading.

Gaia immediately wished she had worn something a little less street rat chic, **inconspicuous** then immediately hated herself for having the thought.

GAIA STOOD IN THE MOST INCONSPIC-
uous corner of Sideburns
Tim's apartment and watched
the door, silently cursing Ed
Fargo's name. Had they or had
they not said they would be
here at eight o'clock? She'd
even swiped one of Ella's

Gaia
Possessed

watches to make sure she'd be here on time. That
was the last time Gaia would ever even
consider being considerate.

There was something weird about this party. It was
different from the last, and only, party she'd been to
since she arrived in New York. The lights were dim.
The music was low. Scented candles dotted the room,
lending a heady aroma. Everyone seemed mellow.
Comfortable. Cozy. It made Gaia want to crawl out
of her skin. She gripped her water glass as if it were
the only familiar object in the room.

"Gaia Moore?"

The grip on the glass tightened dangerously. It
took Gaia about three seconds to recover from the
surprise of someone actually saying her name. Of
course, it was Megan Stein. Heather's right-hand snob,
looking oh so fetching in some half-sweater thing over
some half-shirt thing. She was standing there with another FOH, and each of them was sporting
such overexaggerated expressions of

shocked disgust, they could have just walked off a sitcom set.

"What are *you* doing here?" Megan asked, glancing at her friend, who smiled and looked away. Like the remark was so clever, she could barely contain her laughter. Like she really cared about sparing Gaia's feelings.

"Having the time of my life," Gaia answered flatly.

Megan let out a short laugh. "It must be so fascinating to be so weird," she said, looking Gaia up and down. Gaia immediately wished she had worn something a little less street rat chic, then immediately hated herself for having the thought. She placed her drink down on the glass-topped table next to her. When her inner Gaias were having conversations among themselves, it was definitely time to bail.

"Leaving?" Megan asked, arching one eyebrow.

Gaia wasn't about to waste another syllable on the girl. She pushed by Megan and her silent partner. She could practically feel the cold outdoor air on her skin. The second she hit the street, she was going to find a pay phone, call Ed and ream him out, then call Mary and tell her not to bother leaving the house. What was she thinking coming here, anyway? Did she think she was going to have fun? At this point, it was pretty obvious that on top of being less one fear gene, Gaia was also missing the gene that allowed enjoyment of life.

"Aw, look," Megan said from somewhere behind her. "We scared her away."

Stopping in her tracks, Gaia felt her hands ball into fists. Ignore her. Ignore her. Ignore her. Megan wasn't worth it. Heather, maybe, but not Heather Junior.

"Want me to kick her butt for you?"

Gaia glanced over her left shoulder. It was a guy. Tallish. Asian. Black hair almost hardened by gel. GQ handsome. Definitely Young Entrepreneurs of America. Definitely not the type of person who usually talked to Gaia of his own volition.

"What?" Gaia said, narrowing her eyes.

He walked over, brushing Gaia's arm with his own, and leaned one shoulder against the wall, crossing his arms over his chest. He studied Megan from across the room. "Because I think I could take her," he said. "I'm stronger than I look."

Flirting. Did everyone know how to do this but her? "I don't know," Gaia said flatly, pushing her hair behind her ears. "Girls like that have this habit of scratching. It's not pretty."

He laughed, and Gaia almost looked behind her to see who'd caused his mirth. But then she realized he was looking at her, his black eyes shining in the soft light. So he thought she was funny. Wittiness had slipped from her tongue.

"You should stay," he said, reaching past her to a bowl of peanuts on the counter. He grabbed a handful and cracked one open, letting the little shell shards pepper the plush burgundy carpet. He lifted his chin in Megan's direction. "She's a messy drunk. In about an hour I'm sure we could convince her to strip or chop off all her hair or something."

A short laugh bubbled out of Gaia's throat, and the guy smiled. She felt her face turn bright red. Had she been partially possessed or something?

"What's your name?" he asked, munching on a peanut and holding out a handful to her.

Gaia took one and crushed it in her fist, adding her debris to his. "Gaia," she said.

He glanced at her peanut crumblings with an impressed smirk and held out his hand. "Charlie," he said. "You have no idea how nice it is to meet you."

THE REFLECTION WAS ALL BLURRY.

The Unattainable

Heather couldn't decide if she was drunk or if the Racenellos needed to remodel their bathroom. She turned on the faucet, stuck her hands under the water, and immediately pulled them away.

"Ow. Hot," she squealed, holding the side of her hand to her mouth and sucking on the reddened skin. Then she laughed. "Definitely buzzed," she told herself. She smiled contentedly. It was nice to be buzzed.

Heather was about to turn toward the door and go when she heard a faint pounding. She paused and squinted around. Where was that coming from? She padded across the large bathroom, looking at the ceiling, the tub, the tiled walls. Then suddenly the glass shelves rattled, and Heather jumped.

"Oh, Michael."

It was faint, but she heard it. Accompanied by another rattle of shelves. Heather laughed and covered her mouth with one hand.

"They're having *sex*," she whispered incredulously, her eyes wide. As if she didn't know half the bedrooms had already seen a ton of action tonight. She tiptoed over to the wall and put her ear to the cold tile. Somehow she could only hear less that way, so she pulled back again.

"Baby, you're so hot," Michael said. Heather almost gagged. How cheesy was that? Whoever that girl was, she should wake up and smell the bad cologne. The guy probably didn't even know her name if he was calling her baby.

That was when the moaning and intermittent yelping started, and Heather couldn't take it anymore. She lunged for the door and ducked out of the bathroom into the crowded hallway. A short guy who was definitely going to be balding in about three years was leading a giggling freshman down the hall toward Michael's Boudoir of Sex.

"Don't go in there," Heather warned as she shuffled by. "Give them, like, half a minute. He should be done by then." Then she cracked up at her own joke and kept walking, ignoring the couple's curious stares. Heather felt pretty good, especially considering her little encounter with Sam. She hadn't even thought about him once since she'd been here.

It probably helped that Gaia hadn't had the guts to show after all. If Heather had laid eyes on Gaia, she would have to be reminded of Sam. And how his eyes had finally focused at the mention of her name. And how the thought of Gaia going to a party had made him so jealous, his nostrils had actually flared.

Just as Heather hit the crowded living room, someone grabbed her arm and spun her around so fast, it took the rest of the room a few seconds to catch up with her. It all slid into focus and bounced to a stop like a ball on a roulette wheel.

"You're never going to believe who's slumming with Gaia Moore." It was Megan's voice. Her face wasn't all sharp yet, but it was definitely her voice.

"She's here?" Heather said, feeling the mixed drinks start to remix themselves in her stomach.

"Yeah. And she's talking to Charlie Salita," Megan answered, almost sounding pleased that she was the one who got to deliver this mind-bending news. Her little tendril curls bounced so crazily around her face, it made it all the more difficult for Heather to focus.

Heather turned, slowly this time, and scanned the fuzzy-figure-filled room. Sure enough, Gaia Moore was leaning against the far wall, looking `like a homeless shelter reject`, laughing it up with Charlie Salita, who was looking like he'd just stepped off a Milan runway. Charlie Salita. The unattainable. The only guy Heather had ever liked that she had never gotten to kiss.

Charlie laughed. Heather's stomach turned. It was either flee to the bathroom or the bar.

Heather chose the bar, although she was pretty sure she was done drinking for the night. She found a stool and plopped down next to one of Charlie's friends—a semicute jock named Scott Becker.

"Can I get you a drink?" Scott asked, leaning toward her and grinning.

"Uh, just a water. Thanks." Heather threw one last glance in Charlie's direction, but she was determined to at least *look* like she was having a good time. When she turned back around, Scott was still grinning and holding a beer in his left hand.

"Thought you might like a beer instead," he

whispered, nudging her. Something in his smile put Heather on edge.

"Whatever." She shrugged, taking the beer and sliding off her stool. As she started making her way back toward Megan, she looked over her shoulder toward Scott. He was scowling at her back as she walked away. What a creep, she thought to herself. Heather Gannis knew when a guy was trying to get her drunk. And Scott Becker had picked the wrong girl to take advantage of, she mused, as she took a sip of her beer.

GAIA WATCHED AS CHARLIE PLACED

Actual aughter

a peanut on the dining-room table and crouched down. He brought his eye level with the top of the table and studied the crowd as if he were lining up a cue with the ball. Then he reached up, pressed the tip of his thumb and forefinger together, and flicked. The peanut flew off the table and pelted some kid in a plaid shirt with a choppy haircut on the back of the neck.

He flinched, reached back to touch his wound, and

turned around, glaring in Gaia and Charlie's direction. "What are you—"

"Duck!" Charlie whispered. Before Gaia could even ask him why they should bother, he grabbed her wrist and tugged her to the floor. His face was inches away from hers as he laughed like a little kid who'd just found a dollar on the sidewalk. He had good teeth but onion-dip breath.

"Do you think he saw us?" Charlie asked, pressing one hand against the carpet to keep his balance.

Gaia rolled her eyes. "No. We're both invisible, actually."

"Your turn," Charlie said, pressing a few sweaty peanuts into her palm.

"I don't think so," Gaia said. "You've already taken out most of the room." She suddenly wished Mary *had* shown. Fun didn't get much cleaner than using Planters' Best as miniature weapons. And she had a feeling Mary would have perfect aim.

Charlie bit his lip and grinned. "Come on," he whispered. "There's gotta be someone you want to peanut pelt."

How about half the world's population? Gaia reached above her head and opened her fingers above the edge of the table, rolling the peanuts onto the thick surface. Then she pushed herself up on her knees so that just the top of her head was visible over

78

the table. She scanned the room for her target, found her mercifully close by, and took aim.

Charlie popped up next to her just as the projectile nut hit Heather right on the cheek.

"Ow!" Heather protested, slapping at her face.

"Nice!" Charlie whisper-shouted.

Gaia cracked up laughing and rolled under the table. Charlie was practically crying from the effort to hold in his mirth.

"I didn't actually just do that," Gaia said, holding the heel of her hand to her forehead.

Charlie shrugged. "I'm buzzed—what's your excuse?"

Gaia had a slew of great excuses. She was obviously being controlled by an alien race. Or Ella had slipped some kind of upper into her water. Or she was asleep and dreaming. It had to be one of those because laughing wasn't something Gaia did in real life. Almost ever.

"Do you think it's safe to stand up?" Charlie said.

"Whatever," Gaia answered, pushing herself to her feet. She looked around, expecting the dagger glare, but Heather was off in the corner, flirting with some kid with an underdeveloped goatee. Interesting. Did this mean that Sam was a thing of Heather's past? The possibility brought yet another smile to Gaia's lips. Somebody should be writing this down. Recording it all for posterity.

Gaia Moore. Monday, November 30. Five-plus

smiles. Actual laughter. Subject obviously acutely disturbed.

"You have an amazing smile," Charlie said, his voice so close, Gaia almost thought it was coming from inside her own head. She was surprised when it sent her heart racing. Her mind searched for something to say. She was sure there was a proper response for something like that, but it wasn't anywhere in Gaia's memory banks.

She just stopped smiling.

"Do you want to go somewhere?" he asked, looking out at the crowd as Gaia followed his gaze. The plaid shirt guy was still eyeing them suspiciously. "Somewhere where the natives aren't out for blood?"

Stuffing her hands under her arms, Gaia glanced at Charlie. His sparkly eyes had turned serious. He didn't want to get away from the natives. He just wanted to get her alone. Even someone as inexperienced in romance as Gaia could figure that one out. But being alone with him was out of the question. There was no telling what she might manage to do wrong.

"I . . . uh . . ."

Yet another situation with no ready response. Gaia looked at the door, the hall, the window. At all places leading out. They each looked really far away.

Glancing at Charlie, Gaia was hit by the sudden

urge not to hurt the feelings of the third person who'd been nice to her since she'd come to the city. Stranger still, she also realized some small part of her wanted him to continue wanting her. He was nice. Funny. Cute. Uncomplicated. And he seemed to like her. Gaia Moore. The freak with the huge shoulders and the even huger thighs.

Gaia racked her brain for a graceful bow out. She came up blank. When was she going to wake up and start watching soap operas instead of *Scooby-Doo* reruns?

Somehow "Shaggy! Run!" didn't seem appropriate at the moment.

ABOUT FIVE SECONDS AFTER ENTER-

Bliss

ing Tim's apartment, Ed was convinced that the Tin Man from Oz didn't know how good he had it. Not having a heart seemed like a huge blessing.

Gaia was standing about ten feet away from him, and she was smiling. At Charlie Salita. Charlie every-girl-in-this-room-has-wanted-me-at-some-point-in-her-life Salita. The guy was wearing a brown chenille turtleneck and black pants with highly shined black shoes.

He made Ed look about as sophisticated as Elmo.

Ed was about to cut his losses and maneuver his chair around—no easy feat on carpeting that was about three inches thick—when he heard the most beautiful sound ever to float past his eardrums.

"Fargo!"

It was Gaia Moore, spitting out his name.

"Hey!" he said, looking up as Gaia stalked across the room toward him, leaving a baffled-looking Charlie in the dust.

Ed didn't care that Gaia looked like she was out for blood and that she could probably crush his fingers with a flick of her hand. He steeled himself for the onslaught of blame. He was over an hour late. He knew it. He was willing to accept his punishment as long as it kept Gaia away from Charlie the Suave for a few seconds.

"I know, hit me," Ed said when Gaia reached his side. "Let me have it. I know you hate me."

"Thank God you're here," Gaia whispered, glancing at Charlie over her shoulder. "Can we go now?"

"Hey! Gaia the Brave!" Tim Racenello sauntered up to Ed and Gaia and handed each of them a beer. "Hey, Shred," Tim greeted Ed, chucking his chin in his direction.

"Hey," Ed said, forcing a smile. Had it escaped Tim's attention that he'd just interrupted the nice little triumphant moment Ed had been having?

"So, Gaia," Tim said, shaking his hips comically and dancing right up to her. Ed almost cracked up at the unabashed look of irritation on Gaia's face. A look that Tim, of course, was oblivious to. "Want to dance?" Tim asked.

Gaia reached out, took Ed's beer, and placed it with her own on top of the stereo console at the end of the hallway.

"We're leaving," she said, swinging around to face the door. Before Ed turned to follow her, he saw Tim's face fall so quickly, it defied the laws of physics.

And that was when Ed discovered what bliss felt like.

From: Maryubuggin@alloymail.com
To: Gaia13@alloymail.com
Time: 8:05 P.M.
Re: re: tonight

hey g!
    i'm in! i'm in! but I can't get there till late. my dad has this business dinner thing and the client's bringing his son and my dad is just so incredibly sure that we'll hit it off he can barely keep the sadistic smile off his face.
    right. I mean, the man means well, but the last son of a millionaire had back hair and an excess of toe cheese.

don't ask me how I got close enough to find that out.

anyway, I won't be there till around 10:30-11. hope you're still there.

see ya!

mary

There was
kissing.
That much
she
remembered.

tired

heather

HEATHER LEANED AGAINST THE wall in Tim's hallway, staring at the white front door of the apartment. She wasn't sure why she was staring at it, but she'd been doing it for so long, she was sure there was a reason. If she could only re-member . . .

More Here Than Sam

"Heather?"

She moved her head too fast, and her eyes started to swim around in their sockets. Heather giggled. She felt like a fish in a very round bowl. She reached out and grabbed her friend Laura's arm, although she wasn't sure if it was Laura, or Megan, or someone else entirely who had said her name.

"Hey!" Heather said, rubbing the sleeve of Laura's sweater between her thumb and forefinger. "This is *really* nice."

"Are you okay?" Laura asked, pulling her arm away. Heather just stared at it.

"Yeah. Did the door, like, do something to offend you?" Megan asked, scrunching up her entire face so that she looked like a cartoon version of herself. "You looked like you wanted to kill it or something."

"I'm waiting for Sam," Heather said, blinking. At least she wished she was.

Megan's eyebrows shot up. "Sam's coming?"

"No."

"Oh."

Megan and Laura exchanged pitying looks that Heather wasn't about to stand for. These two were boring her, anyway. She had to find someone to talk to. Someone who wouldn't constantly remind her that she was supposed to have this perfect boyfriend as part of her supposed perfect life.

"I have to go," Heather said, walking along the wall away from them. She stumbled over her own feet and heard Laura and Megan giggle but ignored it. Like they were ones to talk. How many times had she walked them home, stopping every few feet so they could vomit in the sewers? She was allowed to get drunk every once in a while. Although she wasn't sure exactly how she'd gotten *this* drunk. She'd finished off the beer that Scott had given her and decided to call it a night, but somehow her head was now spinning out of control.

Where was Gaia? Where was the bitch hiding? Heather suddenly felt an intense need to tell the girl off. More intense than the usual, day-to-day, moment-to-moment need, anyway.

Heather took her hand away from the wall for a moment. Bad idea. Then someone walked into her shoulder, hard, and Heather decided that the wall was the safest place for her, at least until she found someone to talk to.

When had this party gotten so crowded? Everywhere Heather looked, there was an unfamiliar face, and the place was starting to get unbearably hot. Probably because of the smells. All kinds of scents—perfume, colognes, alcoholic beverages, processed food, and smoke—were choking the oxygen out of the room. They seemed to make the place even warmer, combining to form a thick cloud that locked in the heat like the greenhouse effect.

Air. Air would be good.

"Hey, Heather."

She looked up to find Charlie hovering next her, a semiconcerned smile on his lips.

"Where's Gaia?" Heather blurted out, forgetting momentarily that she was having breathing issues.

"I think she left," Charlie said, leaning one shoulder against the wall. He took a sip of his beer and grinned at her, his eyes sparkling. "Doesn't matter, anyway. I've been wanting to talk to you all night."

"Really."

It was a line. Even through her inebriation, she could spot that one from a good ten yards. But it didn't matter. Gaia had obviously pulled a Gaia and done something repelling to scare Charlie off. Why Sam was immune to her freakishness was beyond Heather.

Sam. What was going on between him and Gaia? It was something. She knew there was something on his side because he'd told her. Actually *told* her. But was there something actually *going on*? And if so, was it something big? Or something minuscule? Was it even real?

"Heather?"

No. It was real. It was in his eyes. Her eyes. Maybe Gaia had gone to find him. Maybe they were hanging out together right now. Kissing. Holding hands. Laughing at her.

Maybe they were in love.

"Heather?"

"Do you want to go somewhere?" Heather asked, her eyes truly focusing for the first time in over an hour.

Charlie's smile was practically blinding. He really was hot. Hotter than Sam, maybe. Certainly more wanted than Sam. Certainly more here than Sam.

"I have the perfect place." There was a flash of something in Charlie's eyes as he said it. Something disturbing enough to make Heather's heart skip a quick beat. But it was just a flash. And it was just Charlie. And Heather just wanted to get out of this room. He held out his arm, just like an old-fashioned gentleman, and Heather only stumbled a little as she took it.

GAIA COULD HAVE SWORN SHE smelled the gas before she even heard the crash. She and Ed had just made it across Fifth Avenue when a moving truck skidded through a red light and fishtailed, taking two cabs and a VW Beetle with it. There was a huge cacoph-

Fifteen Minutes

ony of screeching metal, shattering glass, and earsplitting screams and then an odd sort of silence.

"Oh my God," Ed said, his voice sounding like it came through a black tunnel to reach her ears.

That was when she heard the baby wailing.

Ed grabbed at Gaia's fingers, probably predicting what she was about to do, but she twisted out of his grip easily. She busted through a group of onlookers, half of whom were gaping, the other half helpfully dialing 911 on their cell phones.

"Huge truck—"

"Fire starting—"

"Get an ambulance here as—"

A few words repeated themselves in Gaia's mind as she skidded toward the crumpled, flipped silver Beetle.

Gas. Fire. Baby. Mother. Explosion. Orphan.

Gaia hit the ground on her knees, ripping gaping holes in her pants. The grit and slimy grime of the street pressed their way into the wrinkly flesh around

90

her knees, along with a few pieces of glass. Some part of her brain registered the fact that that was going to hurt later. All she could consciously deal with at the moment was the sight of a red-faced, screaming baby, relatively unharmed, hanging upside down in his car seat.

And the sight of a woman, knocked out, bleeding from the forehead, pressed at an impossible angle against the roof of the car, her arms flopped over her torso like a rag doll's.

"Lady!" someone yelled from the side of the street. "Get out of there! It's gonna blow." The voice sounded panicked. Gaia knew she was probably about to die, but it didn't hit her. Nothing ever hit her the way it was supposed to.

Gaia stuck her hand under the woman's nose, fully expecting to feel the cold absence of breath but instead feeling a little burst of warmth. She was still breathing. Good. But the baby had to come first. Gaia flipped over onto her back and shimmied her way through the smashed window of the car, sliding along the inside of the roof.

It was a close fit, but she managed to cram her body under the screaming child. She held his stomach with one hand, and unhinged the tiny cloth belt on his seat with the other. Cradling the wailing baby against her chest, Gaia slowly squirmed her way back out the window.

Luckily there was a cop standing right over her, panting. His face was determined, but his skin was sallow.

"Give him to me and get the hell out of here," the tall, burly cop said.

Gaia handed him the baby and immediately crouched down to work on the mother.

"Girlie," the cop spat over the screams of the baby and the wail of too distant sirens. "There's gas. There's fire. How stupid are you?"

Stupid. Crazy. Fearless. It was amazing how the interpretations varied.

"So go," Gaia said, reaching into the car and grunting as she worked at the twisted mess. There was no more blood, which made Gaia feel a little better about her prospects, but the buckle seemed to be jammed.

"You're crazy," the cop said, before turning on his heel and fleeing. Gaia could smell the gas. She could hear the fire and feel its heat. Desperate yells and screams rang out from the side of the road, the loudest of which was Ed's. And the sirens grew louder and more persistent every minute, piercing her head with sharp slices of pain.

But she ignored all of it. She had to. It was the only way she could work.

Gaia jammed her thumb into the belt button with every ounce of strength one digit could contain, and it finally popped free. The woman slumped even farther. Gaia reached out a hand and cradled the woman's head.

She heard a popping sound and briefly wondered if that meant the whole car was about to burst into flames. Would that be the last sound she ever heard?

The woman moaned, and Gaia grabbed her under the arms, pulling her free from the car. The woman's heel caught on a chip of glass. It pulled off her shoe, and a long gash opened in the flesh around her heel.

The woman didn't seem to feel it, so Gaia ignored it as she dragged the woman across the street at a run. As she got closer to the sidewalk, a large man in a business suit and overcoat came out and took the woman up in his arms.

"Inside," he told Gaia, nodding toward the Pier 1 Imports store, where a couple dozen people were ducked behind furniture, trying not to look at the wreck. Gaia saw Ed staring at her from behind the counter, his eyes full of fear, anger, and gratitude.

Gaia opened the door, the man ducked in with his burden, and the whole sky turned to flames.

There were more screams. A shower of glass. Still outside, Gaia felt the thrust of heat and turned to look at the road, watching as a puff of flame and smoke rose up from the Beetle in a cloud that extinguished itself as quickly as it had appeared.

It was actually kind of cool. Like a Fourth of July firework.

Before Gaia could even register how sick it was that

these were her thoughts at a time like this, she was bombarded by more people than she ever wanted in her personal space.

"Are you insane?"

"How did you do that?"

"Do you want to go out sometime?"

"Hey! There's the news van! Over here!"

As Gaia wiped the itchy sweat from her brow, she caught a glimpse of a big blue van with a huge antenna screeching toward the scene of the accident. The Pier 1 crowd was gesturing wildly for the driver's attention, clamoring for their fifteen minutes and wanting to thrust Gaia's upon her.

There was a bright white light. A couple of flashes.

"Ed?" Gaia yelled, searching the crowd for him.

"I know," he said, right at her elbow. "Let's go."

THERE WERE JUST WAY TOO MANY piles of clothing on Heather's bed. When she'd walked into her room after midnight on the night of the party, she didn't even have the energy to shove them all to the floor, so she lay down on top

Almost Abused

of them—face first. She felt like someone had hit her with a steamroller, backed up, and hit her again. Twice.

"Tired Heather," she croaked into her pillow. "Very tired."

Something was stabbing her in the stomach. Just a belt buckle. Or a hanger. Nothing compared to the overall ache that was crushing her into her center.

Her throat was incredibly dry, and her face felt like it had been rubbed down with sandpaper. Raw and itchy. Heather rolled over onto her back and felt like she was leaning on a small pillow. It took her a few seconds to realize it was her hair, tangled into a knotted ball at the top of her head. She gingerly touched her hand to it. That was going to hurt like hell to brush through. She tried to kick off her shoes, but her legs yelled out with pain, her thighs quivering like she'd just run a couple of miles.

"Don't move," she told herself. "Better not to move."

Better not to move so that she could think. Lie here and think and try to remember how, exactly, she'd ended up having sex with Charlie Salita.

There was kissing. That much she remembered. Lots of tongue and saliva. Groping. She'd even been quite helpful and popped open the ever-male-confounding front closure bra for him. He'd had a very smooth chest. Smooth and muscular and brown.

And there were a lot of pillows. Flowery ones with this ugly purple pattern that made it look like the Fruit Of The Loom grape guy had barfed all over the bed.

Bed. Okay, she remembered that, too. Heather squinted at the stucco ceiling, her eyes playing games with the swirly patterns and making her whole body spin. She felt very nauseous. Very spent. Almost abused.

She'd had a crush on Charlie in the eighth grade, worshiped him from afar in the ninth grade, almost gotten him to kiss her in the tenth grade, and then been totally humiliated and heartbroken when he'd told her he just wanted to be friends. A teenage boy who refused to even kiss her and leave her. Hormones didn't even play a role. Very ego damaging.

It was a long, sordid history of daydreams, doodled hearts, and tears.

She was a senior now. She had a boyfriend.

Maybe.

She didn't care about Charlie anymore.

But she wouldn't have minded being able to remember the sex.

THIS WAS SUPPOSED TO BE A PARTY?

The Big Ten

Mary Moss had never seen anything so pathetic in her life. A couple of kegs. A few tonsil hockey games. Bad music-store-compilation CD. It was no wonder Gaia thought this would be funny. These people must have learned how to party by watching reruns of *The Wonder Years*.

A dorky guy with a completely over-it Caesar haircut sidled up to her and held out a beer. "Night owl." His head bobbed up and down like it was hanging from a piece of elastic. "I like it," he said.

Mary took the beer, chugged half of it, and handed it back. "Do you know Gaia Moore?"

His eyes roamed up and down her body, and he leered a smile. "Of her," he said.

Suppressing an eye roll was almost painful. Mary's consistently small store of patience was nigh gone. "Is she here?"

"Saw her somewhere," he said with a little shrug. What she was actually there for obviously had no bearing. All he could see were the possibilities. Little did he know there were none. "Why don't you come sit down?"

"No, thanks," Mary said. "I wouldn't want to bother you. I can see you're really busy wasting space."

His face registered no recognition of the insult, so Mary just snorted and walked away. This was a big apartment. There had to be someone here who had a line of coke or some real alcohol.

Wait, no. Not anymore. This was good, clean fun night. As much as she wanted drugs, as much as her body craved them, she was determined to follow through on her promise to herself.

It didn't matter, anyway, right? At this moment she'd settle for the stimulation of a lot of chocolate and a good game of Twister.

Mary made her way down a freshly painted hallway, pausing to listen at doors as she went. Nothing. Nothing. Moaning. Fighting. Nothing. Obviously Gaia hadn't gotten her message and had been intelligent enough to recognize lameness run amok when she saw it. Maybe it was time to go home and relax with Conan and a really big pillow.

Suddenly a burst of loud laughter made Mary jump, and a slow smile crept across her face. Finally. She fluffed her long, curly red hair, straightened the shoulders of her black leather jacket, and pushed through a large swinging door.

The kitchen was huge. White. Immaculate. There was a raucous group of testosterone-high guys standing in the corner, bent over the table. One of them seemed to be taking notes in a big, cloth-bound book. No one noticed her.

This was obviously some kind of meeting. She obviously wasn't supposed to be part of it. That obviously meant she was going to stay for as long as possible. Mary tiptoed past a sparkling butcher block and ducked behind a counter. Perfect view of the guys, but they couldn't see her unless they were looking for her. Or the dog food that, from the smell of it, she was hiding behind.

"What about you, Charlie?" the guy with the book asked, rolling his pencil end over end between his fingers. "Add to the grand total?"

"Only one tonight, gentlemen," the Charlie guy answered. He was one of those guys who was totally aware of how good-looking he was, thus making him entirely unattractive. There was a round of disappointed, jeering "ohs" from the crowd, and a bunch of the guys laughed. Charlie held up his hands and backed up a step, smiling the whole way. "Wait, wait, wait. She's a Big Ten."

The "ohs" turned to "ooos." Impressed glances all around.

"This I gotta hear," the note keeper said, leaning back in his seat and pushing up the sleeves of his off-white sweater. His beady little eyes were shining with interest, piquing Mary's own. Charlie was obviously a big manly man among the manly men.

Charlie looked around, as if checking to see if he had the full attention of his audience. Once satisfied, he opened his arms and gave a little bow. "Heather Gannis," he said with false modesty.

Mary knew Heather. If she was a big anything, it was a big bitch.

"No way!" some kid in a hideous lounge shirt shouted, thrusting his arm down like a kid who'd just been picked last for kickball.

Charlie grinned. "And boy, can that girl move." More laughter, catcalling, and applause from the crowd. Bad shirt guy shot an icy glare at Charlie from the other end of the table, never taking his eyes off the victor as he took a long swig from his bottle.

Mary felt her face go red as the reality of what these guys were discussing sank in. The disgust mixed with the pungent aroma of the dog food made her stomach crawl.

"You got a confirm on this?" Notebook Boy asked, his pencil now poised over the open page in front of him.

A short kid in the corner raised his long-neck bottle of beer. "I saw them go in, and she looked very happy when they came out."

"Five points for Charlie," Notebook Boy said, making a note in his tome with a flourish. "For bagging a Big Ten."

"To the Big Ten!" the short guy yelled. He was answered by a chorus of echoes, more applause, and another bow. That was when Mary couldn't take it anymore.

"Was it your total lack of decency that brought you guys together, or do you all just have really small penises?"

There was a brief, confused silence as Mary stepped out from her hiding place and into full view in the middle of the kitchen. A few jaws dropped and a few sets of eyes narrowed before anyone spoke. It was Charlie who finally processed what she'd said. Mary was surprised that he was the one with half a brain.

"Who the hell are you?" he asked, sounding like a B-movie cliché.

"Who cares who she is?" the note keeper said, standing up and squaring his shoulders, all menacing-like. "What matters is how much she heard."

Mary rolled her eyes. "About what?" she scoffed, tossing back her hair. "Your pathetic little sex ring? I heard enough to tell all your conquests about it."

The guys exchanged looks, clearly trying to figure out what to do about her and her threat. Mary's heart suddenly started to pound out of sync with its normal rate. There actually were a lot of big necks, large hands, and teeny-tiny intellects in the room. Plus they were a bunch of sex fiends. Not exactly an ideal place for an attractive girl like herself to be making challenges.

Charlie finally emerged from the group and started in her direction. Mary fought the urge to back up and raised her chin. She couldn't remember the last guy who had intimidated her. Or at least the last guy who had gotten any indication that he'd intimidated her.

Of course this was one damn big guy backed up by about fifteen others.

"I'm giving you five seconds to get out of here," Charlie said when he was close enough for her to smell the Tic Tac-tinted beer stench on his breath.

Like that was supposed to scare her.

"And you won't be telling anyone anything," he added. "We're not afraid to hurt girls." He actually smiled as he said this, causing sweat to pop out in the center of Mary's palms with a maddening itch. "Got it?" he asked with a very serious edge in his voice.

"I got it," Mary said, surprised at the strength in her voice as she looked into a pair of very disturbed eyes. She glanced around the room, making sure to look at every single face so they would know that she wasn't, in fact, squirming.

The final look of disgust was saved for Charlie. She managed to hold it for a couple of seconds even though he was still glaring at her, and then she turned and went back the way she came, whacking open the door with a flourish.

It wasn't until the elevator doors had slid shut behind her that she let herself realize her knees were shaking.

I have my weaknesses. Things that make me lose my focus. Things that make me impossibly angry. Things that make me see red.

I only had the one tonight. Only the brunette. The blond slipped through my fingers. I don't know how, but she did.

That's one of the things that brings the fury, the not knowing. Being unable to pinpoint where I went wrong. What she saw or didn't see. Whether I said too much, too little, exactly what she didn't want to hear.

It's the not knowing that kills.

But I will have her. I will figure her out. None of them are that complex.

Not a one.

It wouldn't
be Ella's
fault if
Sam, say,
stepped in
indispensable
front of a
speeding cab,
would it? Or
a subway
train.

The Word

ELLA STARED OUT THE PLATE GLASS window of the loft in Hell's Kitchen, watching steam billow out of a manhole in the middle of the street. The image left her feeling cold. Cold and angry. Ella hated the winter. Had ever since she was a girl. There was something suffocating about it. The thick clothes. The tight spaces. The holiday crowds.

It made her feel small.

"You know, I've had people shot for not listening to me."

Ella snapped to attention at the sound of the word *shot*. He would do it. She knew that. She wasn't as indispensable as some.

She turned from the window and faced Loki. His eyes, as always, were unmasked. Sinister. But there was laughter in them. He didn't really intend to kill her. At least not today.

"I'm sorry," Ella said, running the tip of her finger along the edge of the galvanized metal counter next to her. The one that held the plans. "I was distracted. It won't happen again."

Loki's mouth twisted into a smirk. "Daydreaming about the holidays, are we?" he asked. "Or are you just thinking about what will happen to you if I find out you're lying about our unfortunate friend, the doctor?"

They'd been over this already. Several times. And although Ella had been frightened when Loki first confronted her about the doctor, the explosion, and what part she'd had to play in the whole fiasco, she was now getting a little bored. Of course Loki had found out about the events of the last few days. When it came to anything having to do with Gaia, Loki always found out. He knew about the explosion; he knew that Gaia had been at the station that night; he knew that a girl had been brutally slashed; and he knew of the doctor's unfortunate—and obviously more than coincidental—demise. He also knew that Gaia had ended up in the hospital.

The one thing Loki couldn't know for sure was what Ella's involvement had been. Loki was a master of information, but Ella had covered her tracks well, and she was a good liar. After all, she'd learned from the best. And although Loki was obviously still suspicious, Ella knew it was in his best interest to give her the benefit of the doubt for now. She *was* dispensable, but it would be very inconvenient to get rid of her. Besides, he could have no idea that Ella's hatred for Gaia went deeper than petty rivalry. He couldn't know that she wanted nothing more than to see Gaia dead. And his ignorance of that one simple fact was probably the only reason Ella was still alive.

Loki spread a blueprint out on the drafting table in front of him. Ella glanced at the corner of the page and noted the label New York Department of Public Works. It was amazing how Loki could get his hands on whatever he pleased.

"Sugarplums dancing," she said flatly.

"How is my Gaia?" Loki asked, studying the plans, oblivious to the fact that the mere mention of the name brought most of Ella's blood vessels dangerously close to bursting. "Is she excited about the holidays?"

Ella shrugged. "I don't know how she feels," she said, trying to keep the bite from her tone.

Suddenly Loki turned on her with the speed of a wildcat, his eyes crazed with anger as he thrust a crumpled-up newspaper into her face. "You don't even know what she's *doing*," he growled, baring his teeth just slightly.

Ella's life stopped flashing in front of her eyes when she realized he wasn't, in fact, holding a weapon. Shaking, she gingerly took the newspaper from his hands and unfolded it. There was a large black-and-white photo of a twisted car wreck, accompanied by a headline that made the blood in her veins run cold.

MYSTERIOUS BLOND WONDER GIRL SAVES BABY, MOTHER

Finding her voice somewhere among the confusion her insides had been twisted into, Ella tried for an excuse. "We don't know that it was—"

"Of course we know it was her!" Loki spat, the rims around his eyes just a slightly darker shade of red than his skin. "Why didn't you report this?"

There was no way she could tell him she didn't know. No way she could tell him she was home, cleaning up the muck that passed for dinner in the pit that passed for a home where she lived a life that passed for a life with a man who could have been her father. And she was doing it all for him.

She couldn't tell him that.

"The girl is fine," Ella said slowly, realizing she was actually unable to recall whether or not she'd seen Gaia since she left the night before. "I didn't want you to worry unnecessarily."

He glared at her. "You're skating on thin ice, Ella."

Ella blushed, feeling like a small child who had just been reprimanded for skipping her homework. She hated being made to feel like this. Hated Gaia for being the cause.

Loki took a deep breath and let it out slowly, audibly, through his nose. "From now on I want to know everything," he said, his mouth turning into a sly grin. "I don't need your protection."

"Yes, sir," Ella said. And he turned back to his plans as if nothing had ever happened.

"What else has our Gaia been up to?" he asked, his gaze flicking over the numbers printed at the edges of the large page he was studying.

Our Gaia.

"She's going to parties," Ella said, lacing her fingers together behind her back to keep her hands from clenching into fists. "And she's been with that boy," she added, mostly to see if he'd react.

She wasn't disappointed.

Loki turned to her, one eyebrow raised. "Has she?" He seemed to be contemplating the news. Gaia getting too close to Sam could be risky for Loki. Ella knew this. It was only a minuscule risk, but still, Loki had gotten rid of people for less.

Ella was practically salivating. All he had to do was say the word, and she would gladly execute the job. In the most painful and messy way possible.

"Good," he said finally.

Ella almost choked. That wasn't the word she was looking for.

"I'm sorry?" she said, before she could think the better of it. But Loki was flipping through his plans, apparently willing to ignore the fact that she'd questioned him. His mood swings were completely unpredictable.

"If he makes her happy, good," Loki said, frowning as he leaned closer to the desk, tracing one of the hundreds of jumbled lines on the blueprint with his nail. "Maybe she'll stay out of trouble until I need her."

Need her. That stung. Ella was so sick of hearing it, she could scream. What could Gaia possibly do for him that she couldn't do? That she hadn't already proven she was willing to do time and time again?

"Ella!" he roared. Her heart hit her throat so fast, she coughed. Now his eyes were smoldering again. "Don't make me tell you a third time," he said. He thrust his finger at the plans. "There is work to be done."

Ella shoved images of Gaia and her little friend aside and joined Loki at the drafting table. She would have to deal with Gaia and Sam on her own, that much was obvious. Loki might want Gaia to be happy, but it wouldn't be Ella's fault if Sam, say, stepped in front of a speeding cab, would it? Or a subway train.

But whatever she decided to do, the planning would have to be saved for another time.

If she wanted to live long enough to follow through with it.

SAM FINISHED REVIEWING CHAPTER

seven of his physics book and tossed his mechanical pencil down on top of a pile of dog-eared notes. His eyes were dry, and he felt **Stirring** like he hadn't blinked in hours. Actually, it was quite possible that he hadn't. Physics was just that riveting.

Rubbing the heels of his hands into his eyes, Sam leaned back in his desk chair and sighed. He had about eight more chapters to go through, and his energy stores were sapped. If he looked at one more equation, he was going to snap and do something stupid. Like run through the hallway naked, singing Backstreet Boys songs at the top of his lungs.

Some guy on his hall had done that during midterms. It wasn't pretty.

Sam knew from years of cramming experience that there were three options for restoring his brain to a functional level.

One: caffeine

Two: sugar

Three: exercise

And since exercise could translate into a walk, which could possibly lead to seeing Gaia, Sam opted for number three.

He pushed away from his desk, grabbed his worn wool coat, and was out on Fifth Avenue in thirty-five-point-three seconds, departure time hindered only by a slow elevator. Sam took a deep breath of the crisp afternoon air and turned his footsteps toward Washington Square Park.

With any luck, Gaia would have ducked out of lunch for a quick game with Zolov and he could get a dose of her. Something to tide him over until finals were a thing of the past and he could see her again.

What a joke. Sam knew that if he saw her, it would only make things worse. It would only make it that much harder to work. He shoved his freezing, chapped hands into his coat pockets. He knew he should turn around and head home, but he didn't. Instead he walked directly through the arch at the top of the park and immediately started his search.

He knew it was bad for him, but he couldn't help it. He was a Gaia addict, and this might be the only place he could score a hit.

But it was possible to take Gaia in moderation. Sam nodded as this thought occurred to him, making him feel slightly better about his mission. He could just stand across the park and watch her as she anticipated her next move on the board. He could at least see for himself, with his own eyes, that she was okay. That would be enough.

Or would it?

Now that he'd felt what it was like to have Gaia in his arms, would anything less ever be enough?

He could talk to her, maybe. If he could get his voice box to work in her presence, which almost always seemed to be a problem.

As long as she didn't haul off and punch him, he could, in fact, kiss her.

Maybe that would help. If he did, maybe he'd see that

it was just another kiss and not the mind-blowing, shiver-inducing, skin-tingling event he'd imagined it to be.

And then he saw her. And all the blood in his body raced into his heart. It was just the back of her head. The tangled blond hair. It had such an effect on him, he almost had to sit down.

This was bad. Very, very bad. If seeing the back of her head did this to him, what would seeing her face do? Her eyes. Her mouth. Hearing her voice. Sam suddenly knew for sure that if he went over to the table where she was sitting, probably lightening the wallet of the guy across from her, he would never be able to walk away.

It would be impossible. Gut-wrenching. If she gave him any indication that he could have her, he would flunk out of college before he could say "obsessed."

Still, of course, he found himself walking toward her, his eyes trained on the little space of her back and shoulders visible over the top of her chair. In moments he was right behind her. He could practically feel her concentration as she focused on the chessboard in front of her. The guy she was playing was so engrossed, he didn't look up as Sam stood there, hovering like some lunatic.

He opened his mouth to speak, but nothing came out. Probably because he had nothing to say that didn't sound ridiculous.

"Hey, Gaia. Did you know we kissed?"

"Hey, Gaia. How's that head wound?"

"Hey, Gaia. Will you marry me?"

His stomach suddenly wanted to exit through his lips.

Sam snapped his mouth shut, turned on his heel, and forced himself to walk away. It was the hardest thing he'd ever done in his life. But already he knew he'd be useless at his desk for at least a few hours.

He couldn't afford actual interaction. Even if he had left his heart on the ground under her chair.

THERE WEREN'T MANY CLASSES THAT

were easy to handle in the midst of a monster hangover, but the worst was undoubtedly AP biology. Dissecting a fetal pig **Not Rape** made Heather's stomach move in ways she'd never experienced before. She spent half the class period mentally calculating the distance between her lab table and the garbage can, wondering if her projectile vomit would make it that far.

Megan nudged Heather with her arm, and even the slight movement sent a stabbing pain through

Heather's temple. It was two o'clock in the afternoon. Shouldn't she be over this by now?

"What?" Heather snapped as quietly as possible. More because saying anything louder would cause severe head trauma than from any concern over attracting her teacher's attention.

"Have you talked to Lucy today?" Megan asked, casting a glance in their friend's direction. She was sitting at her lab table, looking like `three-day-old roadkill`, watching blankly as her lab partner made the first incision.

"No, but it looks like she and her mirror had a little disagreement this morning," Heather said flatly. It was a sad day when she couldn't even glean any joy from her own creative insults.

"Come on," Megan said, pushing away from her table. "Crosby's not paying attention. Let's go talk to her."

Heather didn't see why they had to bother, but she wasn't in the state of mind to argue. She followed Megan over to Lucy's table and then trudged the extra steps to the window as Megan pulled Lucy to the wall. Heather slumped against the black counter that ran along the windowsill, hoping Lucy's tragedy, whatever it was, merited only a short story.

As Megan started the ritual poking and prodding, trying to get the sordid details of why Lucy was make-upless and wrinkled, Heather zoned out. All day she'd been getting little flashes of her escapades the night before, and she was still trying to piece it together. Where Charlie had taken her. How she'd gotten there. And why. Only small snippets of the conversation reached her ears.

" . . . thought he liked me . . ."

Typical.

" . . . said I was beautiful . . ."

Shocker.

" . . . said no, like, a hundred times . . ."

Wait a minute.

" . . . I don't know if it was *rape*."

Heather's heart hit the floor, disturbing her already coiled stomach as it went.

"Lucy . . . *what?*" she said, finally focusing on her friend's gaunt face. A horrid pain stabbed at her temples, but she barely felt it.

Lucy seemed to shrink before her eyes, hugging herself so tightly, she could have been wearing a straitjacket. Megan turned to Heather, her eyes wide with disgust, disbelief, and fear over what Lucy had just told her.

"I said, I don't know if it was rape," Lucy repeated, sounding like a timid five-year-old being made to speak in front of the class.

Heather grabbed Lucy's tiny wrists and looked her in the eye. "If you said no, it was rape," she said quietly but firmly. Lucy just blinked a few times, heavy tears

116

filling her already puffy eyes. God, not Lucy. The girl couldn't have been more innocent if she'd grown up on a milk farm in Wisconsin instead of the Lower East Side. She still carried around a Hello Kitty pencil tin.

"Who was it?" Heather asked. Her skin felt like it was tightening over her bones, pulling her in.

Flashes of memory assaulted her brain like a strobe light. Charlie holding her down. Her bruised thighs. The rough, raw skin on her face and neck. His hand on her neck . . . covering her mouth . . .

Lucy just shook her head.

"Lucy—" There was an edge in Heather's voice that she didn't intentionally put there. She suddenly felt like pounding something, but at the same time it was as if her entire body had started to ache.

She remembered how she'd felt when she'd gotten home last night. Raw. Spent. Abused. What if—

"You don't have to tell us if you're not ready," Megan said, shooting Heather a warning glance as she ran her hand over Lucy's fine brown hair. Heather was shaking now. She reached out and grasped the edge of the windowsill, pressing her fingertips into the painted wood. She had to stay composed. She couldn't let them see the wall come down. And it was dangerously close to crumbling.

Charlie. The sweater. The bed. The bra. The pillows. The hands. The bruises.

What had happened between the living room and the bedroom?

She didn't remember saying no, but she didn't remember saying yes, either.

I have spent the past two years turning silence into an art form.

If you told my friends that, they'd laugh in your face. To them, I'm outspoken, opinionated, self-righteous, maybe even obnoxious. Loud in a number of ways. But what they don't know is that my being so vocal masks my silence. The more I say about things that don't matter, the less they know about the things that do.

I don't talk about the fact that my family has no money.

I don't talk about my sister hating school and whining about it all the time.

I don't talk about the hand-me-downs, the scholarship applications, the sublet bedroom in my already tiny apartment.

I don't talk about my problems with Sam, Gaia related or other.

All I talk about is nothing. Lots and lots of nothing.

But this is one thing I don't think I can keep inside. Charlie

may have raped me. But unlike
Lucy, I really, *really* don't know
for sure. I need to talk this
through with someone. I need to
figure out what to do.

Because this is one thing I
can't be silent about.

A girl has to draw the line
somewhere.

She used to sound
like that with
him all the time.
But that was be-
fore. When they

vulnerable

were together.
When they were in
love and it was
safe to be
vulnerable.

WHEN IT CAME TO SCHOOL DAY activities, it took more than a hallway catfight to surprise Ed Fargo. He'd seen a lot in his day. Danny Cicinia putting his fist through a plate glass door, Mr. Weitzman threatening to "toss" Jason Cirelli if he talked back

Couldn't Happen

one more time, Renee Barrow pulling the fire alarm just so she could get thrown out of school in time to make the bus out to the Meadowlands to see Rage Against the Machine.

Still, he was almost shocked into speechlessness when Heather Gannis walked right up to him in front of everyone who was anyone—at least to her—after eighth period.

"Can we talk?" she asked.

Ed would have really preferred not to. Lately, conversations with Heather either involved Gaia bashing or Sam gushing. Two topics Ed wasn't remotely interested in. Plus there was the whole pain-of-talking-to-an-ex thing. That never helped, either.

But one look at Heather's eyes told him not to turn away. She needed him. She had no right to, but that was a discussion for another time.

"Yeah," he said. "Do you want to meet me at Ozzie's later?"

She shook her head almost imperceptibly. "Now," she said.

Ed's brows knitted, and he automatically gripped the armrests on his chair. When Heather turned and headed into their history classroom, Ed followed without hesitation. Something was really wrong if Heather wanted to spend an extra two minutes in the school building after the freedom bell had rung.

As soon as he was through the door, Heather closed it behind him. She leaned back against the gray metal desk at the front of the room and regarded him for a moment, as if she was rethinking her decision to spill. Then, just when he thought she'd changed her mind, she spoke.

"I think Charlie Salita might have raped me," she said. At least that was what Ed thought she'd said. Part of him was now fairly sure he was hallucinating.

"What!"

"Don't make me say it again," Heather said, crossing her arms over her chest and looking away.

Ed knew all the color had drained out of his face and that every pore on his body was producing sweat at profuse levels. This was something no part of him was willing to believe. This couldn't happen. Not between people he knew. Not between people he was friends with. Once.

This couldn't happen to Heather.

"Are you going to say anything?" she asked. For

the first time in recent memory, her voice sounded vulnerable. She used to sound like that with him all the time. But that was before. When they were together. When they were in love and it was safe to be vulnerable.

"Are you okay?" Ed asked, holding her gaze.

"I don't know," she said. She held herself a little tighter. "That's the problem—I don't know anything. I don't remember much."

Ed rubbed his hand through his hair, mostly to clear the sweat that had accumulated on his palm. "What do you remember?" he asked.

He would kill Charlie Salita. He would find a way to get up out of this chair if he needed to, but he would definitely kill the guy.

Heather sighed wearily and dropped into a chair next to him, causing a metallic scraping sound that echoed in the empty room. Ed could see the pores around her nose, smell the sweet trace of perfume that was left from her midday spritzing. It was the closest her face had been to his in years. His heart couldn't help responding with a strong hammering to his chest. He ignored it. This wasn't the time for that.

"More every time I think about it." She started to pick at her nails. They were all chipped and ripped and shredded. Was that from fighting back, or had she destroyed them in the trauma of the aftermath? "I remember him holding my arms down. I remember his hands on my neck. . . ."

As she spoke, Ed started to feel like he wanted to crawl out of his skin. It was like his insides were clawing at him, but he couldn't tell her to stop. If she needed to talk about it, he needed to make himself listen.

"You don't want to hear this, do you?" she said, her tone flat.

Ed coughed. "I'm sorry. No. I'm fine. I just . . ."

"You want to know why I came to you," Heather said, staring straight ahead.

Ed said nothing.

She traced a tile on the floor with the toe of her boot, over and over again, getting faster each time. Ed watched, mesmerized, until she pressed her palm into her thigh, holding her leg in place.

"I didn't know what else to do," she said.

Ed's dark half wanted to tell her to go to Sam. That Sam was her choice. That she wasn't Ed's responsibility anymore. But the dark half's voice was weak and irrational. It wasn't who Ed was—most of the time.

"You have to tell someone," Ed said, fighting the urge to reach out and take her hand. If he touched her, she might shrink away. The emotions in the room were so raw, he wasn't sure if either one of them could take that. "I mean, someone other than me. Someone who can do something. The police or a guidance counselor or something."

"I don't want to," Heather said quietly. "At least not yet. Not until I'm sure."

Ed's heart clenched even tighter. She was broken. Charlie had broken her.

"How are you ever going to be sure?" Ed asked, trying to keep the rage and confusion he was feeling from coming through in his tone.

Heather rested her elbow on the desk in front of her and pushed her hand into her hair. "I don't know," she said, sounding a little desperate. "But you'll help me, right? Figure it out?"

He'd never seen so much trepidation in her expression. Not even right after the accident, when things had gotten intense in a bad way. It took more guts for Heather to be this openly confused than it ever took for Ed to surf the biggest wave in the ocean.

"I'll help you," he said, and before he could stop it, his hand reached out and covered hers. They both just looked at it for a moment. Ed marveled at how it hadn't changed—the look of her skin against his. It felt different, but it looked just like it always had.

"And you won't tell anyone?" she asked.

"I won't."

But Ed's other hand was hidden at the side of his chair, and his fingers were crossed. A childish gesture he hadn't used since the third grade, but then, a lot of things were happening today that hadn't happened in a long time.

Heather didn't want to involve the police until she was sure, but Ed knew of only one way to find out. Get Charlie to confess.

And he knew of only one person who could do that. And it was the last person Heather would ever want knowing her secrets.

Gaia Moore.

ELLA KNEW SHE WAS SUPPOSED TO

be working, but she consoled herself by remembering that Sam was part of all this. Loki might not think he was important right now, but Ella knew better. He was important. One day Loki would thank her. Commend her for her foresight.

When Sam left his dorm, Ella tailed him without much care for discreetness. He wasn't trained to spot her, so there was no reason to put in the effort. She knew where he was going, anyway. To the park, to look for Gaia.

How pathetic could he be?

Still, he was nice to look at. The way the late afternoon sun highlighted his hair and the shape of his cheekbones. Ella wouldn't mind getting a piece of Sam Moon.

Which was exactly why Gaia wouldn't be.

Ella would make sure of that.

She followed him across Washington Square North and through the arch. He stopped to help a little girl who'd dropped her books pick them up and replace them in her bag. So he was chivalrous, too. Did the fun ever stop?

Ella kept walking, deciding to find a perch in the park where she could keep an eye on him while he kept an eye out for Gaia. Loki would have wanted Ella to be keeping an eye out for Gaia too. But right now that didn't matter. Right now, she was working for herself.

AFTER SCHOOL GAIA HEADED STRAIGHT for the park as fast as her tattered sneakers would carry her. She felt the need to reimmerse herself in the world she loved.

A Threat

In the society of other social abnormalities like Zolov and Renny and Mr. Haq. Last night she'd come far too close to the normal high school experience for her own comfort. And this lunchtime's game with the Wall Street dork had done nothing to stimulate her brain cells.

It was time for a freezing-yet-challenging game of chess and some conversation with a little old Russian.

And if she bumped into Sam while he was on a study break, well, that wouldn't technically be her fault.

Gaia was just blowing by Tower Records when she could have sworn she heard someone call her name. The wind was definitely playing tricks with her. She kept walking.

"Gaia?" Jogging footsteps. "Hey! Wait up!"

She stopped and shoved her hands in the pockets of her sweatshirt jacket. As she turned, the wind blasted into her face, instantly watering up her eyes and practically tearing her hair out of her scalp as it whipped back.

"Are you crying?"

It was Charlie Salita. And he looked genuinely concerned. Go figure.

"No," Gaia said, touching her raw palms to her eyes. "Just the wind."

"Oh." He smiled. His smile really didn't suck. Gaia suddenly felt totally conspicuous, standing on the street corner with one of the Village School's elite. She was already getting sucked back into the social black hole. "Where are you headed?" Charlie asked.

Gaia pointed her thumb over her shoulder. "Park."

"Cool. Mind if I walk with you?"

He had to be kidding. Wasn't it illegal for him to be seen with her or something? Weren't there universally accepted rules about this type of inter-high-school-species fraternization? And she couldn't believe he hadn't been totally put off by her hasty retreat the night before. There was something very odd going on, and Gaia wasn't entirely sure what to do about it.

Avoidance seemed like a good plan, though.

"Do you want something?" she asked, starting off. He fell into step beside her as she crossed Washington Square West and headed into the park. He had a long stride and kept pace with her easily. Most people had to jog to keep up.

"No," Charlie said with a laugh. "Why do I have to want something?"

Gaia glanced at him out of the corner of her eye. "Most people do," she said.

"Okay, I do want something." He stopped and backed out of the walkway so that the other pedestrians could get by. Gaia hesitated for a moment, then backed off the path in the other direction. She faced him, but there was a steady stream of people bustling by between them, trying to get to their next destinations before their noses froze off.

"What is it?" Gaia semishouted.

"Can you come over here?" Charlie said, clearly amused.

"Whatever it is, you can ask me from there," Gaia said. She was bouncing up and down on the balls of her feet, trying incredibly hard not to scan the area for Sam.

"Fine. I was wondering if you would go out with me this weekend," Charlie shouted. A couple of younger kids going by on skateboards snickered and leered at her as they passed. As her face turned an extremely dark shade of confused red, Gaia had three simultaneous thoughts.

Charlie was brain damaged—which wasn't all that shocking.

She was flattered—which definitely threw her.

And there was no way she was ever going to say yes.

There was the whole interspecies thing. The whole date-awkwardness thing. The fact that the last guy she'd said yes to had turned out to be a serial killer.

And there was also Sam. Or at least the possibility of Sam.

"I don't think so," Gaia said, starting off toward the chessboards again. Thankfully, Charlie didn't follow this time. He didn't drop it, either.

"I don't give up that easily!" Charlie yelled after

her. He sounded very happy about it. Like he'd just made the ultimate promise.

Unfortunately, to Gaia it sounded more like a threat. She was actually starting to like the kid a little. It would be a pain if he kept forcing her to say no.

THE ASIAN BOY LAUGHED AS HE

pulled on his leather gloves and strolled out of the park, right by Sam. Right by Sam, who had just narrowly missed the little shouted proposition.

A Rift

The flirtatious smiles. The flattered blush on Gaia's face.

Ella had to sit down.

Why did he have to stop for that little girl? That could have been such a satisfyingly awkward confrontation. It might not have caused a rift, but it could have caused a crack. A splinter. A little hairline fracture.

It would have been entertaining.

Ella glanced from Gaia's face back to Sam's. Each going off in an opposite direction. They'd missed each other. At least that was something. And it would have to be enough.

For now.

SAM WAS VERY PROUD OF HIMSELF.

Beautiful Choice

He'd managed to walk right through the park to the other side in a straight line without even glancing at the chess tables. He'd been very good. He definitely deserved a lollipop or something.

He walked down Broadway into the heart of Greenwich Village, finally allowing himself to glance around as he went—checking out the bizarre array of people milling all around him. A fake blond in a power suit walked by a guy playing a pair of metal garbage cans like drums on the sidewalk. Then a homeless woman hobbled past, yelling at him for making so much noise, and an obviously stoned college kid came to the drummer's defense, telling the woman she wouldn't know art if it bit her in the ass.

Sam chuckled and shook his head. *This* was a study break—people-watching in the Village. If anything could clear his mind of equations and formulas, it was this. When he got back to the dorm, he'd be refreshed and ready to focus.

"Watch it! Watch it! Out of the way!"

Sam looked up just in time to jump out of the path of a messenger on a ten-speed doing mach twenty on the crowded sidewalk. He pressed his hand against a shop window to balance himself. There were laws against that these days, weren't there?

Suddenly there was an impossibly tiny Chinese woman getting right in his face. "You get fingerprint all over window!" she snapped.

Flinching, Sam pulled his hand away. "Sorry," he said.

"Get out of here, or you be *very* sorry," the lady warned, scrunching up her face angrily.

Sam took off down the street, shoving his hands under his arms. Suddenly people watching didn't seem very entertaining anymore. He ducked into the first shop he saw, just to get a breather from the bedlam outside.

Once he took a look around, he couldn't believe his luck. He'd fallen right into a specialty shop that sold board games. Lining one entire wall was a glass case filled with all kinds of chessboards, from the simple to the ridiculous. One pitted little metal American presidents against famous foreign leaders of the past. Another had intricately painted Disney characters dressed up as kings and queens and knights. Then there were marble sets and glass sets and ceramic sets. As Sam wandered along the case, he couldn't believe his eyes.

It was like Mecca for chess geeks. He wondered if Gaia knew about this place. He was sure she could spend hours in here.

Suddenly his eyes fell on a small wooden board on the bottom shelf. The squares were made out of dark cedar and light birch, and the pieces were carved down to the most minute detail. The whole thing had been shellacked and shined so that the shop lights bounced off the polished surfaces. It came in a small wooden carrying case that closed with a gold clasp.

The set was made for Gaia. It was beautiful, yet simple, and the girl who always seemed to be on the move could take it anywhere.

Sam rubbed his palms against the thighs of his cords and looked around. He hadn't even bought a Christmas present for his mother yet. Or for Heather. He never shopped until Christmas Eve, when all the salespeople seemed to want to gouge his eyes out just for walking into the store.

Was he nuts for thinking about buying Gaia a gift? He wasn't even totally sure how she felt about him. If he bought this for her, she'd probably think he was an overzealous, clingy freak.

But she would also love it. Of that he was sure. And it would be worth it just to see the look on her face when she held those tiny little pieces in her hand. Another reason to look forward to the end of finals.

A salesman in a maroon sweater vest with a bad comb-over practically tiptoed up to Sam. He placed his hands together and smiled. "Can I help you, sir?" he asked.

"I'd like the travel set," Sam said quickly.

"A beautiful choice," the man said so automatically, it was clear he recited those words about twenty times a day.

Still, Sam grinned as he reached for his wallet. It was a beautiful choice. For a beautiful girl.

WHEN GAIA TURNED ONTO PERRY

Street on Tuesday night and smelled the smell again, she immediately turned around and started back up Hudson. **Threesome**

Her taste buds had already been massacred once this week, and she was too smart to make that mistake twice. Her stomach wanted food tonight, not bark and slop. George was just going to have to suffer without her.

Now came the good part. Deciding among the many fine grease-slinging restaurants of New York City. If there was any pleasure in Gaia's life, most of it came from sampling every fried food and sugar-coated anything on the Lower West Side. She hadn't run out of dives yet, but as soon as she did, she was going to branch out into other neighborhoods. Gaia hadn't seen Mary since she'd missed the party last night, so she'd yet to make good on her promise to help distract her friend. And the hunt for bad-for-you food was always distracting.

She would have called and told her to come down, but Mary had sent her a message this morning saying she was knee-deep in "family stuff" and would call when she could. She'd also included a cryptic p.s. saying that they needed to talk.

Gaia could guess what Mary wanted to talk about. The party had, admittedly, been relatively clean, but as far as "good" and "fun" went, there was no question it was a complete failure. Mary would be chomping at the bit to break the whole thing down into a play-by-play in which she'd find a way to make fun of every single person that was there. As far as "family stuff" went, Gaia already knew that probably meant "getting Mary clean" stuff like family counseling. Ick. Mary had described her program as being a cross between group therapy and Chinese water torture. When the poor girl finally came up for air, at least the party would be something for her and Gaia to laugh about.

Gaia gripped the strap on her messenger bag as she took the wind in the face. She ducked her head and watched the ground as she walked. Another of the many good things about winter. No one felt the need to make eye contact.

As she walked, Gaia passed by some of her

standard favorites. Mama Buddha, where they sold the best wonton soup she'd found thus far. Franco's Gyro, where she knew better than to ask what was actually in the pitas. Before she knew it, she was headed up Sixth Avenue. When she passed by the colorful windows of Urban Outfitters, Gaia realized where her stomach was leading her.

Gray's Papaya. Home of the fifty-cent hot dog. Gaia had at least three dollars in her pocket. It was time to feast.

She mentally congratulated her belly on its choice as she swung open the door to the garishly lit eatery. But the congratulations ended when Gaia saw who was seated at the counter in front of the window along the right-hand wall. Charlie Who Didn't Give Up That Easily and Sideburns Tim.

Her stomach grumbled angrily as she turned to leave. But it was too late.

"Gaia the Brave!"

"Buy you a hot dog?" Charlie asked gleefully. "I swear I won't consider it a date."

Gaia slowly faced them and rolled her eyes.

"Come on," Sideburns Tim said, holding up his orange paper cup. "We'll even throw in a drink."

Quickly Gaia weighed her options. Free hot dogs and annoying company or twigs and slop and even more annoying company.

Too bad there wasn't a curtain number three.

"Fine," Gaia said, plopping onto a stool. "Get me three, with everything. And a root beer."

Charlie and Tim exchanged half-amused, half-disgusted glances, and then Charlie got up to place the order. Sideburns Tim smiled at her as he took a sip of his soda. Gaia stared at her translucent reflection in the plate glass window. Her hair was a brilliant conglomeration of tangles and knots, and one side of her jacket collar was rolled under while the other stood straight up.

She was utterly hopeless.

"I like a girl who can eat," Tim said, wiping his hand across his mouth.

"Pardon me while I swoon," Gaia said, nonchalantly straightening her collar. Tim laughed, and she almost smiled. Another key comeback. She was getting better at this. It almost made up for her utter lack of hygiene.

"So did you ask her yet?" Charlie demanded when he returned a moment later, slapping a paper plate full of hot dogs and relish and every other condiment known to man in front of Gaia. Charlie's hair, on the other hand, was so ordered and flawless, he could have had a team of stylists in his back pocket. He straddled the stool between Gaia and Tim and looked back and forth at them.

Great. What were they going to ask for, a threesome?

"No. She was busy lampooning me," Tim said with a good-natured laugh.

139

Charlie rolled his eyes. "Fine, I guess I have to do everything myself." He swiveled on his stool so he was entirely facing Gaia and popped his feet up on the bottom rung. "We're having another party tomorrow night," he said. "My place this time. I'd love for you to come."

Gaia smirked. "You just want me there for my aim."

"Not my primary motivation," Charlie said.

There was something in the way he said it that made Gaia blush. God, she hated that. Couldn't she have been born without the blushing gene? "I don't think so," she said. Then, as an afterthought, she added, "Thanks."

"Why not?" Tim asked, popping his head up over Charlie's shoulder like a parrot. "Didn't you have fun last night?"

Gaia shoved half a hot dog in her mouth, letting a blob of relish hit the floor. The word *ladylike* wasn't in Gaia's personal dictionary. She was kind of hoping her ickiness would drive them away, but they only looked more fascinated. "It's just not my thing," she said through a full mouth of food.

"Well," Charlie said, eyeing her plate. "We have three hot dogs' worth of time to convince you."

Gaia narrowed her eyes and shoved the other half of her hot dog into her mouth.

Charlie's brow knitted in concern. "You think you could eat a little slower?"

To: gaia13@alloymail.com
From: shred@alloymail.com
Time: 4:30 P.M.
Re: 911

Hey, G.—

I left a couple of messages with Ella, but somehow I get the feeling you'll never get them. I need to talk to you. It's kind of important. If you get this, meet me at Dojo's at seven o'clock. I wouldn't ask if it wasn't huge.

Thanks.

Shred

To: gaia13@alloymail.com
From: shred@alloymail.com
Time: 8:05 p.m.
Re: stood up

Hey, G.—

So I guess you didn't get the message. Call me when you get this. I really need to talk to you. I'm sure you can tell by the lack of bad jokes in this e-mail that I'm actually freaking.

Call me.

Shred

She's going to be a challenge. More so than any of the others. I can tell by the look in her eyes. She thinks she's strong, but she's not. She thinks taking a few classes at Crunch will make her invincible.

I can show her what invincible looks like.

I can show her a lot of things.

"Mind your own business, Shred," he said through his teeth. "Or this chair **damn** is going to seem like a **scary** blessing compared to where you'll end up."

GAIA BOUNDED DOWN THE STAIRS

on Wednesday morning, hair wet, clothes half buttoned, late for school as always. She cursed as she slammed her toe into a doorjamb on her way down the hall. It was then that she realized she'd forgotten to put on her shoes.

She came around the corner into the kitchen and stopped, skidding slightly on the freshly waxed linoleum floor. Ed was sitting at the kitchen table, nursing a steaming cup of coffee.

"Morning," Gaia said, walking by him on her way to the pantry. She was only moderately surprised to see him there. There were two amazing things about Ed Fargo. One was the fact that he was a morning person, and the other was that he seemed to think she was one, too.

"Morning," he replied. "George let me in on his way out." She could feel his eyes following her as she crossed the room. He was waiting for her to say something. As always, Gaia was clueless as to what he expected.

"I brought you a bagel," he said. "Tons of butter."

"Thanks," Gaia replied. "It'll save me the huge prep time for cold cereal." He didn't laugh. Odd. Gaia turned on her heel and trudged back to the table.

"You didn't call me last night," he said.

"Was I supposed to?" she asked, taking a bite of her

bagel. The melted butter coated her tongue, and Gaia almost sighed. Heaven.

"I left you about fifty messages," Ed said with a sullen shrug. Gaia raised her eyebrows, and Ed immediately caved.

"Okay, *five* messages," he said, fiddling with the protective plastic top on his coffee.

Gaia glanced at the cordless phone on the wall next to the refrigerator. "The light wasn't blinking when I got home." Not that she'd actually looked.

"I talked to Ella," Ed said, almost apologetically.

Gaia snorted and picked at her front teeth with her thumbnail. "So this is my fault how?" she said.

"Okay, forget it," Ed said, shifting in his chair. Gaia really studied him for the first time—he was pale, and his eyes were rimmed with gray. He also hadn't cracked a joke or offhandedly complimented her once since she'd entered the room.

How insensitive could she be?

"Ed, what's wrong?" Gaia asked, forgetting about her breakfast.

He pushed his chair back slightly and maneuvered it so that he was facing the table straight on. Then he pulled himself up to the edge and leaned his elbows on the clean white surface. Gaia watched his preparations with growing concern. It never took this long for Ed to talk.

145

"There's a rapist at school," he said finally, his eyes almost wary as he waited for her reaction. Gaia felt all the muscles in her body recoil, tightening themselves as if she were getting ready to spring on someone.

"Who?" she asked.

Ed took a deep breath and held her gaze. "Charlie Salita."

Gaia blinked as her stomach contracted. "No way."

"I know it's hard to believe, but—"

"No," Gaia said, shifting in her seat. "I mean it. There's no way he's a rapist."

Ed's eyes widened slightly in surprise, and he studied her for a moment, obviously unsure of how to proceed. In that moment Gaia just wished he wouldn't proceed at all. She could actually see herself hanging out with Charlie, especially after last night, when a couple of hot dogs at Gray's had turned into a couple of hours at Gray's. There weren't many people who could keep her interest for that long. Besides Sam, of course. But most of the interesting stuff that happened between them happened in her imagination.

Gaia's mind flashed back to the night before, when Charlie had bought a few hot dogs and given them to a couple of homeless men outside. He was a good guy. She couldn't be wrong about this.

Not again.

"Gaia—," Ed began again.

"I'm telling you, Ed," she interrupted, her voice somewhere between pleading and demanding. "It's not possible."

ED FELT HIS FACE FLUSH PURPLE,

 Pain

and he pressed his lips together hard. He couldn't believe it. In every scenario he'd imagined for this conversation, he'd never thought Gaia wouldn't even let him talk.

"What do you mean, it's not possible?" Ed asked. "You spend five minutes at a party with the guy and you know him well enough to decide that?"

Gaia took a deep breath and leaned her forearms on the table. "I hung out with him last night, too," she said, causing a pain to sear through Ed, the likes of which he'd never felt before. "He's no rapist," Gaia added. "He's way too normal to have a secret like that." She paused and took a slow bite of her bagel. "He's also . . . nice."

Ed couldn't believe what he was hearing. Had she been brainwashed or something? Gaia wasn't supposed to trust anyone, least of all a good-looking, spoiled, privileged jock like Charlie Salita.

"The person who told me wouldn't lie about something like this," Ed said, trying to remain on the logic tip.

Gaia ran a hand behind her slim neck and massaged the muscles there, shaking her head. "Okay," she said finally. "When did this girl say this happened?"

Now they were getting somewhere. "At the party," Ed answered firmly.

"He was with me at the party," Gaia reminded him. "For more than five minutes."

Ed's lips tightened. "What about after we left?"

"No way," Gaia said, tearing off a piece of her bagel and popping it into her mouth. Suddenly Ed couldn't help thinking she was protesting a bit too much. Like maybe she was trying to convince herself. "He was happy-go-lucky boy that night," Gaia continued. "He wasn't even drunk." She paused and looked out the window, the sunlight slanting across her face and contorting her features. "If he was going to try it, he would have tried it on me."

Ed pushed his hands into the armrests on his chair and adjusted his position, mostly to give himself something to do as he tried to process Gaia's reaction. He'd always thought Gaia was the guilty-until-proven-innocent type. Charlie must have had a serious effect on her. The pain in Ed's chest cut even deeper.

"Why don't you want to hear this?" Ed asked finally.

Gaia's eyes flashed defiantly, as if she'd just received a huge challenge. "Fine," she said. "Tell me what this person said about Charlie. Exactly."

A sliver of doubt passed through Ed's heart. He knew what Heather had told him wasn't going to be very convincing coming from him. Gaia would have to see the pain and vulnerability firsthand. As if that was ever going to happen. Ed heaved a sigh.

"She said she was pretty sure Charlie raped her." Gaia sucked in air and was about to protest, but Ed cut her off. "But there was someone else raped that night. One of this girl's friends. There's more than one. I'm telling you——"

"This other girl said Charlie raped her, too?" Gaia asked.

Ed paused. "Well, no. Just that she was raped, so——"

"So maybe it wasn't Charlie at all," Gaia said, her brow knitted. "If this other girl was raped, she should press charges or something, but until there's something solid against Charlie, I——"

"I don't believe you," Ed said disdainfully.

"Well, what did you expect me to do?" Gaia said, sounding tired.

"Great, so you'll risk your own life to save random people from a car wreck, but you won't even bother to look into something that I'm telling you is real," Ed practically shouted, the veins standing out on his neck and forehead. "Something that happened to someone I actually care about."

Ed's mouth snapped shut, and his face turned red so fast, his eyes started to water. He couldn't believe he'd just said that about Heather. It had been a long time since he'd allowed himself to acknowledge the fact that he cared for the girl.

There was a slight softening of Gaia's features when she saw his face. "Ed—"

"Forget it," Ed said, pushing himself away from the table. He angled his chair at the door. "I *thought* you would trust me," he said. "I thought we were friends."

As Ed made his way down the hall, a thought occurred to him that almost made him vomit on the spot. Heather *should* have gone to Sam. Gaia would have listened to Sam. She would do anything he asked.

Ed had never felt so useless in his life.

At the front door he realized she hadn't even bothered to follow him. From the sound of the silence in the kitchen, she hadn't even moved from her chair. She was probably sitting in there right now, munching happily on her bagel, totally unaffected.

While Heather was over at her apartment, unable to even think of food.

Ed pushed his way outside into the frost-filled air and took a good, long breath. It looked like he was just going to have to deal with this himself. He looked down at the wheels of his chair and sighed.

Somehow.

ED WAITED UNTIL AFTER STUDY HALL,

The Accusation

when everyone else was getting out of gym, to make his move. He figured Charlie would be all winded and tired from working out for an hour, and Ed would at least hold the advantage of having his wits about him. Of course, there was also the possibility that working out would have Charlie pumped, adrenaline ready to explode.

Why didn't this occur to him until he was sitting outside the locker-room door?

The class started to empty out, and every time the door was flung open, Ed's heart caught in his throat as he waited for Charlie to appear. Finally the flow lessened to a trickle and no Charlie. Just as Ed was about to give up, Tim Racenello walked out of the locker room, buttoning the top button of his shirt.

"Shred!" he said with a grin. "What's up, man?"

Ed swallowed and pushed himself back so his butt was hitting the back of his chair. "I'm looking for Charlie," he said.

"He's in that health section," Tim said, gesturing at the nearly empty hall. Ed rolled his eyes shut. What an idiot. Every quarter a section of the gym class had to take a class in teen health issues. That meant Charlie was somewhere across the school right now. So much for careful planning.

"Want me to give him a message?" Tim asked, his eyes flicking over Ed.

Suddenly Ed had an idea. Tim was Charlie's best friend, and they were nothing if not loudmouths. It was quite possible that Tim knew about everything that had happened between Charlie and Heather. It had happened, after all, in Tim's apartment.

"Yeah," Ed said flatly, glancing over his shoulders to make sure no one was around. Empty. "You can tell him to stop raping people."

ED KNEW HE WAS BEING BLUNT. He knew he was going for shock value. But he never could have been prepared for The Change

152

the change that came over Tim's face when his words sank in. It looked like there was a string attached to his chin and someone was pulling down on it, drawing all of Tim's features closer together. His lips folded into a V, his eyebrows almost touched, his eyes were like slits, and his pupils shrank to the size of pinpricks. His chin even seemed longer.

It was pretty damn scary.

The Real Threat

"YOU KNOW CHARLIE," THE NEW Tim-thing said in a voice that sounded oddly normal. "He wouldn't hurt a fly."

Ed pushed his chair back a few inches to alleviate the disconcerting feeling that Tim was hovering over him. "Look, Tim," he said. "All I know is that someone said—"

"Whoever this someone is," Tim said, crossing his arms over his chest and standing up straight, "she must have wanted it." His features seemed to return to normal as he said the last few words, as if the cliché was comforting to him.

"Tim, this girl is telling the truth," Ed said, feeling

153

more comfortable now that Tim no longer looked like an angry bat. "She's not a liar."

"Heather Gannis not a liar? That's a laugh," Tim said, cracking himself up.

Ed felt suddenly dizzy. "I didn't tell you who I was talking about," he said.

This didn't even faze Tim. He gradually stopped laughing and smirked at Ed. "You didn't have to," he said. "Charlie told me all about it."

"So you knew," Ed said slowly. The ice in his heart was slowly moving to his extremities, `freezing his fingers`. He was sure it would have frozen his toes, too, if he could feel them.

"I knew they had sex," Tim said, adjusting his backpack and looking off down the hall as if he had better places to be. "And I knew she was all over him. He didn't rape her, Ed. Come to grips with the fact that your ex is a slut."

Ed had to hold on to the chair to keep from launching himself at Tim. He knew he'd just fall in a `limp pile` at the guy's feet, which definitely wouldn't get him anywhere. But letting him talk about Heather that way practically killed him. "You come to grips with the fact that there's some evil shit going on at those parties of yours," Ed blurted out, glaring up at Tim with a rage that could have flattened the entire school. "You have to put a stop to it, Tim. He might have done it to a lot of other girls. You never know—"

"And you never know when to shut up, do you?" Tim asked, leaning into Ed's chair. He gripped the armrests, placing his hands just behind Ed's, and brought his face within millimeters of Ed's. "Mind your own business, Shred," he said through his teeth. "Or this chair is going to seem like a blessing compared to where you'll end up."

The bell rang, but Ed barely even heard it over the blood rushing through his ears. Tim straightened up, popped a piece of gum into his mouth, winked, and walked away.

Ed didn't even know what period it was anymore. He had no clue where he was supposed to be. All he knew was that he had to get to a bathroom. Fast.

GAIA WALKED INTO THE CAFETERIA

Loner

and quickly glanced over the crowd. She'd already decided she was ditching out on lunch today, but there was something she needed to get out of the way first.

She plunged into the seat-searching crowd and maneuvered her way over to the table by the window where Charlie and Tim were sitting with a bunch of their friends, some of whom had fallen victim to her projectile peanuts a couple of nights ago.

They were both surprised to see her, so she got to talk first.

"So, I'm in," she said, focusing on Charlie. The sweet if cocky face. The just slightly overlapped, yet ridiculously white teeth at the front of his smile. Not a rapist. Ed must have misheard. Misunderstood. She didn't care. She knew who she was dealing with.

"You're in," Tim repeated, glancing at the other guys around the table. A couple of them snickered and looked away. So juvenile.

"Tonight," Gaia said, pushing a strand of hair behind her ear. "I'll be there. Where's your place?"

Charlie finished chewing on a soggy-looking fry and pulled another little flyer out of his bag. This one was yellow with a cartoon of a little kissing couple.

"Oh, how sweet," Gaia said, stuffing the flyer in her back pocket. "Later." She turned and headed into the crowd again, ignoring Charlie as he called after her to join them. Screw Ed and his bogus accusations. His little speech that morning had reminded her of why she had sworn off friends in the first place. Too much pressure. It was like he thought he could use her as his own personal superhero. He got an idea in his head, and she was expected to follow through with it or what? He wouldn't talk to her for the rest of the day?

Gaia shot a look at their regular table and saw Ed immediately look away. Apparently that was the punishment.

What was the point?

Gaia took the steps in the stairwell three at a time and burst through the heavy metal door onto the street. Automatically her feet started to turn toward the park, but she stopped herself, reaching out to grip the wrought iron fence that ran along the sidewalk in front of the school.

What was the point of going there? Another good question.

Sam wouldn't be there. Sam hadn't called. He hadn't written again after his original, blow-off e-mail. Hadn't called to clear up the mystery of what had or hadn't happened on Thanksgiving. `Didn't even have the courtesy to let her know whether she was still Gaia the Unkissed.` There was no reason to torture herself by going to the park. She was a sorry case for thinking about it. She'd already wasted enough of her life pining. Obsessing. Daydreaming.

Gaia started off in the other direction, sure she could find some distraction farther downtown.

She didn't need Ed. And she didn't need Sam. Gaia Moore was a loner. She did what she wanted when she wanted.

It was time she started to remember that.

The Big Ten

10. Christina Perraita

9. Tashana Rydell

8. Amy O'Neil

7. Caitlin Alesse

6. Michelle Sussman

5. Kim Goldberg

4. Jen Rinsler

3. Jen Malkin

2. Heather Gannis

1. Gaia Moore

The guy
hovering
above her
was taking
off his
jacket
and going
for his
zipper.

**the
attack**

MARY QUICKENED HER STEPS AS SHE
turned off Barrow onto Hudson and
started to walk uptown. She'd chosen
a far too flimsy jacket, which she
pulled more tightly around herself as
the signal at the corner turned red.
She'd lived in New York all her life,
but it never ceased to amaze her how

Falling Apart

she could be perfectly comfortable on one street, turn
a corner, and be freezing. The city was a climactic
anomaly.

It was early, but she couldn't wait to get to the club
and get all sweaty and gross on the dance floor. Mary
much preferred hot to cold. She knew it was dangerous, going out with these friends to this place. She
knew there would be temptations. But she could handle it. She could. All she had to do was think of Gaia.
Think good, clean fun.

She'd yet to have any since she and Gaia had made
their pact. Her first try had entailed staring at mutts
while they tried to hump each other and getting
threatened and the most nonpartyish party she'd ever
come across. Mary was beginning to think "good,
clean fun" was an oxymoron, but she would give it the
old Mary Moss try. At least one more time. Mary took
a deep breath and forced herself to smile. It was all
good. She was going to be just fine without the coke.
Perfectly, perfectly fine.

Making the left on Jane Street, Mary was suddenly aware that the two guys walking behind her were the same two guys who were walking behind her back on Barrow. She hadn't gotten a good look at them, but they stood out because they were walking so close together and she hadn't yet heard them say a word. Her heart started to pound a little faster. She suddenly didn't like the feel of this.

She slowed her steps, hoping they were just a couple out for a walk and were just too in love for words. Maybe they would get frustrated at her pace and pass her by.

Which was exactly what they started to do. Big sigh. Mary stepped left to let them pass. And that was when she saw the masks.

The scream came out without her even willing it, but a large, gloved hand slapped over her mouth and practically twisted her head off as it pulled her back. Mary struggled, reaching her arms up over her head and scratching at his ski mask as the attacker pulled her down a set of darkened stairs.

She kicked out her legs, causing them both to stumble, and they crashed down into the little concrete cove in front of a basement apartment.

Mary had just enough time to register that the door was boarded up and the place was abandoned and that there would be no help before the masked guy backhanded her across the face. She tasted the blood before she even felt the pain pop behind her eye. Then he planted a fist in her gut.

Doubling over, Mary crumpled to the ground. She had to cough, but her body wouldn't let her take in enough breath. Something sharp was cutting into her leg, and she could feel the blood spreading out over her skin, sticking to her tights. It was warm, and it brought her to her senses.

Enough to realize that the guy hovering above her was taking off his jacket and going for his zipper.

The terror that seized her heart was almost enough to kill her right there. But instead it seemed to take control of her body and tell it what to do. Mary quickly rolled over onto her back, lifted her bleeding leg, and delivered one hard kick to the masked guy's balls.

He let out a primal grunt and went over, falling right on top of her, his elbow grinding painfully into her chest. Mary struggled to get out from under him, which wasn't that hard this time since he was totally incapacitated. He fell over onto his side, holding his groin and sputtering a cough.

As Mary struggled to her feet, she scraped both knees against the concrete but barely felt it. She was too busy checking out guy number two through her throbbing eyes. He had his back to them, standing watch. Apparently he expected a loud struggle because the fight hadn't even caught his attention. But Mary running past him would certainly turn his eye.

How the hell was she going to get by him?

And what if she didn't? Was he going to rape her when his friend was done? Was that the plan? The thought sapped Mary's strength, and her knees started to shake as hot tears blinded her vision. She was falling apart. And that scared Mary even more than the situation. She never fell apart.

Suddenly two arms grabbed her from behind, and Mary let out another scream. She reached back with her one free hand and scratched the guy's forearm as hard as she could. Her nails came back with skin and blood packed under them. He yelled out and dropped her. Mary immediately sprang to her feet, taking the steps two at a time.

The watchdog was just coming to the top of the stairs when she got there. He was big. Bigger than the attacker below, but Mary had two things going for her. Adrenaline and speed. She rammed into the guy's shoulder, sending him reeling backward in obvious surprise.

Then she ran, tears streaming down her face as she barreled by shoppers and theatergoers and drunks. Part of her wanted to go right home and hide under her covers, but the rational part of her brain kicked in and told her she was miles from home. She'd have to wait for the subway. They could follow and catch up to her, and who knew what they'd do to her now that they were pissed.

When she got to Perry Street, she hooked a left.
She just hoped Gaia was home.

GAIA HAD YET TO ANSWER THE

doorbell at George and Ella's
house, but there was a first
time for everything, and she
was sort of standing in front

Paralyzing

of it. Avoidance was almost impossible. But when she
swung open the door, she immediately forgot about
the novelty of it all.

Mary was standing there, looking like she'd just
clawed her way out of the grave. There were cuts,
bruises, blood, dirt, dried tears. A crushed
cigarette butt hung from a tangle in her matted red hair.
For a moment Gaia forgot where she was.

"Can I come in?" Mary asked. Her voice sounded
like someone had rubbed her throat down with sandpaper. She pulled her hair back from her face, revealing more bruises, and shook the cigarette away, the
effort almost bringing her to tears.

Gaia stood aside, holding the door open farther. As
Mary entered the foyer, Gaia heard Ella stirring in the
office.

"Can you get up the stairs?" Gaia asked, glancing

toward the back of the house. Ella was closing drawers, putting things away. Any second she would walk out, and she would definitely want an explanation. She'd probably toss Mary out on the street before she'd risk getting blood on any of her "neocolonial" furniture.

"I think so," Mary croaked.

"Then let's go," Gaia said. She hustled Mary up the stairs, moving her faster than was probably comfortable for her. It was painfully, painfully slow to Gaia, but it was fast enough to get her friend out of Ella's sight in time.

"Gaia?" Ella called up after them. "Who was at the door?"

Normally Gaia just wouldn't bother answering, but she didn't want Ella coming upstairs and banging into her room again.

"Girl Scouts!" Gaia called back. "I put you down for a dozen boxes."

Mary stumbled into Gaia's bedroom and sat down hard on the floor, wincing in pain. Gaia slammed the door shut behind them and joined her friend, sitting Indian style on the hard wood.

"What happened?" Gaia asked, trying to keep from staring at Mary's wounds. There was a yellowish bruise forming around her left eye, and her lip was crusted with blood.

"Two guys just decided to use me for some recreational

entertainment," Mary answered, gingerly touching a cut on her leg. Gaia reached up onto her bed, grabbed the white T-shirt that was balled up there, and handed it to Mary. Her friend looked at it quizzically.

"It's for your leg," Gaia said.

"It's brand-new," Mary said, holding it carefully away from all the blood.

"It's just a shirt," Gaia answered. She took it out of Mary's hands and held it to her friend's leg. A bright red splotch of blood seeped out across the stark white fabric. They both stared at it for a moment in silence. Gaia could tell by the steadying of her breaths that Mary was taking that moment to calm down. To come to grips with the fact that she was safe.

Gaia was just getting more and more angry.

"Did you get a good look at them?" Gaia asked finally, still staring at the blood. If Mary told her one was blond and one was brunette, Gaia would take out every Waspy guy in the city.

"No, but I took a chunk out of the one who used me as a punching bag." Mary held up her right hand. Three of her fingertips were covered in dried blood. Gaia was glad that Mary had gotten in one good blow.

"They were wearing masks," Mary continued, pressing her hands onto the floor and squeezing her eyes shut in pain as she adjusted her position. She pushed herself up so that her back was leaning against the side of the bed and let out a sigh. "But I know who they were."

Waiting for Mary to tell her was hard. It took away from precious ass-kicking time. But Gaia did wait. Mary needed to put forth obvious effort just to think.

"I went to that party the other night," Mary said finally, glancing at Gaia quickly. "You'd already left, I think."

Gaia felt like someone had just slammed a kick into her stomach. She suddenly had a suspicion about where this was going, and she didn't like it. Her self-flagellation mechanism immediately kicked in, telling her this was her fault. All hers. Somehow everything was her fault.

"I walked in on these guys . . . some kind of sex club or something. They were keeping score," Mary said. She looked down at her lap and picked at the little fuzzies on her sweater. The blood splotch continued to grow on her leg, but her sweater was cleaning up rapidly. "A couple of them threatened me."

"Names," Gaia said, clenching and unclenching her fist. "Did you get their names?"

"Only one," Mary said, looking Gaia in the face. Her eyes squinted, and she bit her bottom lip. "It was Charlie, I think. Yeah. Charlie. He didn't like me very much."

Gaia's vision blurred gray. Her head felt like

it was going to explode. Her fist gripped so hard, her jagged, ripped nails cut into her palm. The anger was almost paralyzing. But it wasn't directed at Charlie now.

For the moment she was angry only at herself.

"ED, WHERE ARE WE GOING?"

Heather asked, sounding weary. She stuffed her hands under the arms of her black wool coat. Her collar was pushed up against the wind, and her hat was pulled down tightly over her ears. You'd think she was on an expedition in Antarctica.

The Old Heather

"You asked me to help you, so I'm helping you," Ed said, bringing his chair to a stop in front of their destination. Bowlmor Lanes.

Heather looked up at the red banner with its big bowling pin and ball. Then she glanced inside at the neon lights and dingy tiled floor. Ed wasn't surprised by the grimace of disgust.

"Help me what?" she asked. "Immerse myself in cheese?"

"Cut the snob act, Heather," Ed said, rolling

through the door and into the waiting elevator. He turned around and looked up at her. "You forget you're dealing with the one person who knows it's faked."

For a split second the mask fell, and Heather stepped into the elevator beside him, but by the time they got up to the lanes, it was back in full force. "Can you even play in that thing?" she asked, eyeing his chair as they approached the counter.

"I can do *lots* of things," Ed said in a little kid voice. Heather cracked half a smile and looked at the big Italian guy who was doling out the shoes.

"Size seven," she said. As he turned toward the wall of shoes, Heather almost grabbed for his arms, then obviously thought the better of it and pulled back. "Clean ones, if you have them," she said. Ed laughed out loud.

By the time Heather had picked out her ball—a purple one, of course—and strapped on her `decid-edly not clean shoes`, Ed had already bowled four balls and hit one strike.

"I can't believe I'm doing this," Heather said, tiptoe-ing up to the line, ball in hand. "If anyone saw me—"

"If anyone saw you, they'd be here, too," Ed said, smiling cockily up at her. "So then they'd pretty much be in the same situation, wouldn't they?"

Heather gave him an oh-aren't-you-so-smart? look and held the ball up to shoulder level. Ed pushed him-self back to give her room and watched her as she studied the lane. She could complain all she wanted, but Ed knew she loved to bowl. She got so competitive, you'd think she was on the Olympic team. If she wouldn't let him help her by going to the police, the least he could do was take her mind off things.

Especially after the way he'd crashed and burned with Gaia.

And crashed, burned, and almost been killed by Tim.

Heather took a few steps, pulled back her arm, and let fly. The ball careened down the lane and smashed into the middle pin, sending the entire set flying. The big dancing X appeared on the screen above their heads.

"Yes!" Heather shouted, throwing her arms in the air.

Ed laughed and automatically held out his hand to her. She slapped it as she strutted past.

"Beat that, Fargo," she said, plopping into an orange plastic chair and crossing her legs in front of her. The waitress came by, and Ed heard Heather order two turkey burgers and two sodas.

"Thanks," Ed said, grabbing his ball and placing it in his lap so he could maneuver to the top of the lane.

"For what?" Heather shouted over the loud music pumping from hidden speakers somewhere over their heads. "Loser's buying, so you'd better find your wallet."

Ed shook his head and pushed his chair forward.

It was nice to have the old Heather back in full force.

Kind of.

"SAM MOON, PREPARE TO DIE!"

Study Break

Sam barely had time to duck under his desk before three of his so-called friends burst into his room and pelted him with water balloons. One splattered against his lower back, dripping ice-cold liquid down his pants and soaking his underwear.

"What the hell are you guys doing?" Sam shouted from the cramped space under his desk. Every part of his body was soaking and stinging except his head.

"Study break, man!" Mike shouted, flinging another balloon. This one bounced off Sam's back in one piece and rolled across the floor. Sam heard a scuffle as Mike and the rest of his friends started to go for it, but Sam was already on the floor, and he was just plain faster. He scurried out of his hiding place, grabbed the balloon, and flipped over into a sitting position, holding it back above his head. His friends all froze, eyeing him warily as they tried to figure out who he was going to decide to attack.

Sam moved the balloon to his left hand and slowly reached under his bed with his right.

"You forget who you're dealing with," he said matter-of-factly, then watched their eyes widen as he pulled out a brightly colored Super Soaker.

"Shit!" they all yelled in unison. They fell over each other as they clamored for the door, and Sam doused them all with one, solid pull of the trigger, chasing them out into the common room. He laughed evilly, drunk with power as they all ducked behind their torn, pizza-stained couch.

"Bow before my greatness," Sam shouted, following up with a cartoon-worthy cackle.

But there was no white flag. Moments later they all popped up again, each holding a balloon in each hand. Sam was toast. His heart actually dropped.

"Put the gun down and back away," Will said slowly.

"I'll never surrender," Sam said, taking a step back nevertheless.

"You will when you see the coolerful we have back here," Mike answered. The boy was very good at menacing. Sam turned and bolted back into his room, slamming the door behind him. He didn't have time to barricade it before they all crashed through. The enduring war was nothing if not disorganized. Everyone was soaking everyone, and Sam laughed harder than he remembered laughing in months. After stressing over finals and Gaia and Heather for the last few days, it felt extremely good to let loose, even if his room was suffering dire consequences.

At one point he finally dared to open his eyes to assess the damage and saw that Mike was about to step on Gaia's gift.

"Stop!" Sam yelled.

Miraculously, everyone froze. Probably because Sam sounded like a borderline psycho.

"Mike, don't move," Sam said, holding out his hand.

"What is it?" Mike asked nervously. "A rat?"

Sam quickly crawled over to where Mike was standing, the knees of his jeans squishing as he went, and gingerly pulled the box out from behind Mike's feet. It was undamaged. It wasn't even wet, which seemed completely impossible. But it was obvious to Sam that he had to get it out of here before the next study break brought an onslaught of food or something.

"Okay, guys, war's over," Sam told his friends as he held the box away from his sopping wet body. "I have someplace I gotta be."

Generally, I'm not a person who plans things. I wouldn't be able to if I wanted to. Make big plans, I mean. I never know where I'm going to be from one month to the next. This time last year, if you'd told me I'd be living in New York, I would have told you to get fitted for a straitjacket.

But here I am.

And I've always been fine that way. Not planning. If you don't figure out exactly how you want everything to be, you can't be crushed when it all goes to hell. So not planning has always been fine.

Until now.

Yes, I can kick Charlie's ass. Yes, I can find out who his little sidekick was and kick his ass, too. I could probably take on their whole little club. But that's not enough. Not this time. I can admit that whatever I can do to them won't be nearly enough. Because with a pack

mentality, there's no guarantee
they won't just get back on the
horse and keep doing what they're
doing.

Bad metaphor.

The point is, this time I have
to have a plan. These guys de-
serve real-world punishment. And
Mary and I both know that with
what she has right now, she can't
prove anything. We have to catch
him in the act.

That's where Gaia the decoy
comes in. I'm the bait. Yippee.

But maybe I can get a confes-
sion out of him—who knows? I can,
after all, be pretty persuasive
when I want to be. That way,
maybe none of us will have to go
to court. Not me. Or Mary. Or
Ed's friend, whoever she was. No
one will have to relive it.

And at the very least, if the
whole plan goes to hell, I'll
still be there.

At least they'll still get
their asses kicked.

Not Gaia. She
was gorgeous.
No makeup. Dirty
hair. Salvation-
Army-worthy **miss**
clothes.
popularity
And she was gor-
geous. Ella
wanted to kill
her.

ELLA WAS SITTING IN THE LIVING

In Charge

room when she heard the door to Gaia's bedroom creak open. Her senses immediately went on high alert. It was her job, after all, to keep an eye on Gaia—to monitor her every move. It was also becoming her obsession.

The sound of footsteps on the stairs was followed by muffled whispers. There was someone with her. Ella pushed herself off the plush, peach-colored couch. If Gaia had smuggled Sam up to her room, there were going to be dire consequences. Ella would have to figure out what they were going to be, but she was confident she could devise some sort of punishment. The girl would have to listen to her at some point. Ella would make sure of that.

She got to the foyer just as Gaia was closing the door behind her visitor.

"Who was that?" Ella snapped, placing her hands on her rounded hips. She so wanted to go over to the window and check the streets, but she knew whoever it was would be far out of sight by now. And she didn't want to give Gaia the satisfaction.

"A friend," Gaia said, her voice very flat. Very low.

"A boyfriend?" Ella asked, frustrated by the high pitch her voice took on. She was jealous. She knew she was. Jealous that Gaia even had a shot at

Sam Moon—that perfect specimen. The jealousy just frustrated her more.

Gaia snorted a laugh and walked by Ella. She ducked into the hall closet, rummaged through it, and pulled out a long, battered army coat. She shoved her arms into it, yanked down on the front of her gray sweatshirt, and checked her reflection in the gilt-framed mirror above the hall table.

Ella watched, almost mesmerized, as Gaia pushed her knotted hair behind her shoulders, licked her fingertip, and wiped a smudge of something from her cheek. If Ella had done that, she would have taken away a fingertip full of foundation and she'd have to start the whole grueling primping process all over again. Not Gaia. She was gorgeous. No makeup. Dirty hair. Salvation-Army-worthy clothes. And she was gorgeous.

Ella wanted to kill her.

"Where are you off to, Miss Popularity?" she asked, crossing her arms over her chest and leaning back against the wall. "You look good enough to go eat out of garbage cans in the park."

"Thanks," Gaia said, buttoning up the coat. "I would go join your friends at the cans, but I have a party to go to."

Ella narrowed her eyes, seeing red as Gaia swept past her, brushing her disgusting old coat against Ella's leg. The girl was so damned cocky. So damned cold and sure of herself. Ella could take that away in an instant. All she had to do was reach into the closet, just inches from where Gaia had grabbed her coat, and get her gun. What Ella wouldn't give to see Gaia's face.

Then Ella would be in charge. Then Gaia would get in line.

And then, of course, Ella's cover would be blown.

"Gaia, you can't just come and go as you please," Ella said, just barely staying in character.

"Watch me." Gaia slammed the door in Ella's face.

For one brief moment there was silence, and then Ella turned and swept the hall table clean, letting out a primal sort of scream. She picked up the largest piece of the now broken lamp and pulled back her arm, ready to hurl it at the mirror. Her reflection looked crazed—frightening—and it gave her pause. But all she had to do was imagine it was Gaia she was looking at, and she snapped all over again, flinging the lamp so hard that for a moment she thought her shoulder had pulled out of its socket.

She smiled happily as Gaia's reflection shattered into a hundred pieces and slipped with a delicious crash to the floor.

One day she would feel what it was like to crush the real thing.

And that day couldn't come soon enough.

GAIA WALKED INTO CHARLIE'S

brownstone and searched the slight crowd from just inside the door. She wasn't even remotely surprised when the lyrics of a familiar Fearless song crooned from nearby speakers.

Ever the Gentleman

Nobody's gonna hold you down. Nobody's gonna make you cry. Nobody's gonna break your heart if you don't let 'em say good-bye.

Gaia smirked at the cliché sentiments, rolled back her shoulders, and headed straight for the far end of the living room, where Charlie was already working his first victim. Some tiny little girl with tiny little arms and tiny little cheeks. Gaia practically shoved her out of the way.

"Hey!" Tiny Girl protested.

Gaia ignored her. The girl could thank her later.

"Hi," Gaia said to Charlie, somehow keeping the disgust out of her voice. He'd tried to rape her friend. Beaten the crap out of her just hours ago. And yet he could stand here in his designer sweater with his gelled hair and his stupid smile and act as if he was God's gift to the female population.

"Gaia," he said with an easy grin. "It's good to see you."

Gaia really wished she could say the same. She'd

really liked the cocky bastard. Enough to go to two, count 'em, two high school parties.

"Can I get you anything?" Charlie asked, glancing toward the makeshift bar at the front of the room.

"Yeah," Gaia said, unable to believe what she was about to say. "You."

Charlie's smile turned into a grin, and it was all Gaia could do to keep from laying him out right there. Instead she lowered her lashes and looked up at him through them, just like she'd seen Heather's flirtatious-by-habit friends do a million times.

"If you're still interested."

Charlie reached behind him and put his plastic cup down on the bookshelf just over his right shoulder.

"Oh, I'm interested." He reached out and took her hand, lacing his fingers through hers. He squeezed. She couldn't bring herself to squeeze back.

"My room's right down the hall," he said, eyeing her as if he was waiting for her to back out. He was in for a big surprise. Or two. Gaia stood up on her tip-toes and brought her mouth so close to his ear, she could smell where the cologne mixed with the gel.

"Let's go outside," she whispered, and almost vomited when she felt Charlie shiver. "I like to do it outdoors."

Not that she had any idea where she actually liked to do it.

But apparently Charlie agreed with her. Before

Gaia could blink, they were halfway to the back door. Charlie, ever the gentleman, grabbed a chenille throw from the couch along the way.

SAM PUSHED HIS HAND THROUGH Something of Him

his hair a few times, hoping he didn't look like a Santa Claus clone with red nose and cheeks from walking in the freezing cold. Gaia's gift, now wrapped with a card stuffed inside, was cradled under his arm. When he got to her house, he was just about ready to puke, but he took the steps two at a time, anyway.

He might as well at least look confident.

The bell played a little tune, but Sam was too distracted to even place it. He took a step back, watching the door as his heart pounded crazily. He heard noises inside and held his breath, hoping Gaia would be the one to answer the door. He wasn't sure if he could handle waiting all over again as someone went off to find her.

A few moments passed, and no one came. Weird. Sam was sure he'd heard noises. He reached forward and knocked. Total silence.

Sam had the sudden, odd feeling he was being watched. He looked up at empty windows. Was Gaia up there somewhere? Had she seen him and decided not to come out? Sam's heart plummeted at the thought. Well, he wasn't going to stand here looking like a moron.

He looked down at the gift in his hands and contemplated it for a moment. Before he could entirely think it through, he bent down and left it on the doorstep. If she wasn't in there laughing at him, maybe she'd get it and get in touch with him.

If she was in there laughing at him, she could have it. The pathetic part of Sam still wanted her to have it.

To have something of him.

MARY HEARD A FOOTSTEP BEHIND

Not Fair

her and glanced over her shoulder for the tenth time in as many seconds. She mentally told her heart to just stay in her throat.

"Just go to the precinct, find a detective, and wait for her call," Mary repeated Gaia's instructions to herself, keeping her head bent against the wind. She watched her feet as they clicked quickly along the sidewalk. There were people everywhere, but Mary felt like she was entirely alone, walking in a spotlight. She was sure they were after her. Every garbage can she walked by hid a masked attacker. Every time she came to an alley, she quickened her pace.

She was starting to sweat under her jacket, and she swallowed hard. When she'd thought about getting hot and sweaty tonight, this wasn't exactly what she'd had in mind.

She hadn't thought that by the end of the night, she'd be afraid of her own city. The town she'd grown up in. The town she'd always loved as her home.

It just wasn't fair. Even less fair was the fact that she couldn't have anything to take the edge off.

"Just go to the precinct, find a detective, and wait for her call," Mary said again, ducking her head even more as frustrated tears burned at her eyes. "Just go to the precinct . . . wait for the call."

"WHERE DO YOU WANT TO GO?"

Charlie asked in what Gaia was sure was his best husky whisper. He sounded like a hoarse dog. Gaia pointed to a relatively clean corner in the tiny "yard" behind

Gaia's Second Kiss

the brownstone. It consisted of a small patch of dirt and an even smaller patch of dead grass. There was a rusted-out barbecue against a splintering wooden fence.

"No one will come out here, right?" Gaia asked, trying to sound like an ingenue.

"Don't worry," Charlie said, leading her to the corner and spreading out the blanket. "I have a friend watching the door." He pulled his sweater off over his head, revealing a T-shirt beneath, and immediately shivered. Still, he tossed it into the corner and ran a hand over his hair. "A little cold out here, isn't it?"

Gaia just plopped down onto the blanket and looked up at him, trying to invite him along with her eyes. She was sure it wasn't coming across because the last thing in the world she wanted was this asshole touching her. She had to remind herself of Mary. This was for Mary and everyone else who hadn't been as lucky as her.

"I guess we'll just keep each other warm, huh?" Charlie said, dropping to his knees.

Gaia tried not to wince as Charlie placed one hand on either side of her body and leaned into her, bringing his lips down hard on hers. She really wished Sam would call and clear up the details of Thanksgiving.

Because she really didn't want this to be her first kiss.

CHARLIE'S LIPS TRAVELED DOWN her neck.

When should she tell him to stop?

He pulled off her sweatshirt, and his eyes hungrily took in the slight tank top underneath.

Making It Believable

Did she have to really get him into it before he would lose it? Before he would be unable or unwilling to stop himself?

He pushed her down against the hard ground, holding her shoulders with his hands as he kissed her roughly.

Okay, that felt like the start of something.

His hand traveled down from her neck to her shoulder and hovered right over her breast.

Gaia pushed him back by the shoulders.

"Stop." Enough, after all, was enough.

"YOU'RE KIDDING ME," CHARLIE SAID.

He was pulling away. Why the hell was he pulling away? Wasn't this where he was supposed to start with the violence?

The Battle of the Stupids

"I—"

"God, Gaia," Charlie said, standing up and grabbing his sweater, which was now covered with dirt. "I never would have pegged you for a tease."

Gaia racked her brain for a response. He was taking no for an answer? This was definitely not part of the plan. She scrambled to her feet as he shook out his sweater. This didn't make any sense. He could grab a girl off the street and try to force her to have sex, but someone teased him into it and said no and he just stopped?

Was she just that bad at this?

The flash of a streetlight on Charlie's silver watch caught her eye, and Gaia instantly remembered Mary's words about the fight. The blood under her nails. Gaia quickly took in Charlie's forearms just before he pulled on his sweater. Not a scratch. He was innocent.

Gaia didn't know whether to be relieved or pissed.

"Charlie, I'm—"

"Save it," he said, grabbing the blanket and heading inside. "You can go home now."

Her eyes narrowed as he walked into the house, letting the door slam behind him. She was glad she didn't get the words out. He was still a big asshole. Gaia picked up her own sweatshirt, desperately trying to come up with the appropriate next move. If it wasn't Charlie, who the hell was it?

It suddenly occurred to her that it could have very well been a random attack. The guys in this sex ring, while being beyond perverted, might not be rapists. Ed could still be wrong. Gaia was completely confused. It was time to grab Mary and regroup.

She was lifting her sweatshirt above her head when she heard the back door close again. Maybe Charlie had changed his mind and decided to jump her after all. Gaia started to turn but didn't even make it all the way around before a powerful punch to the side of her face sent her reeling in the other direction.

Gaia's whole body slammed into the fence, sending a shock wave of pain down her left side and stabbing splinters into her chin. She pressed her hands into the raw wood and started to push herself away, but she was grabbed from behind, spun around, and slammed back against the fence again.

The attacker wasn't that strong, and he was very sloppy. Gaia could have taken him down with any number of her favorite moves. But she wanted to find out who it was first.

His face snapped into focus just as he uttered his telltale greeting. "Gaia the Brave."

She couldn't believe the little runt had the balls.

"Sideburns Tim," she said calmly.

He blinked, obviously confused that she wasn't whimpering, writhing, screaming, and begging. He was probably even more confused when she pulled back and head-butted him so hard that the cracking sound was almost deafening.

Tim slammed into the ground hard and raised his hand to his forehead with a guttural moan. Gaia wouldn't have been surprised if he'd given in right then, but he didn't. Somehow he was on his feet within seconds.

"Gaia the Brave is also Gaia the Stupid," he said, spitting as he said the words.

"Not as stupid as most," Gaia answered. Another cloud of doubt passed over his face, but before it even cleared, Tim lunged at her, grabbing her wrist, twisting it behind her, and sweeping her legs out from under her in one seamless motion.

Gaia couldn't have been more surprised if he'd delivered an expert karate kick to her neck. She was on her face, and his knees were bearing into her back, and she was tasting dirt. Breathing it into her half-crushed nostrils.

"What was that about not being stupid?" Tim said, reaching up one hand to hold her face down. Between the pressure of the ground against her chest and her face full of filth, Gaia could barely take in a breath. And without breath she couldn't fight. She had to strain the muscles in her neck, but she managed to twist her head aside.

She could hear Tim struggling with his belt, the buckle clanging as he undid the closure.

He didn't waste any time, did he?

Gaia twisted her legs to the side and used all the power she had to flip herself over, knocking Tim aside from the force. He was on her again instantly, pushing down her arms.

His belt buckle was smacking against her knees, and Gaia realized he'd successfully pulled down his pants. She couldn't look. He must have had a lot of practice at this to do it that fast. The thought made her ill.

"You're it," he said, his face disgustingly close to hers. "You're the one I need."

For what, she didn't want to know. Somewhere in the recesses of her mind she recalled the fact that in order for it to be actual rape, she had to say no, stop, don't. Say something instead of just beating the guy to a pulp.

"You ready?" Tim asked.

"Don't even try it," Gaia said evenly. "I'm saying no."

Tim smiled gleefully. "That's exactly what I wanted to hear."

He released one of her hands for a split second and went to cover her mouth, but before he got anywhere near her face, Gaia delivered one swift hook to the right side of his jaw and followed it with an uppercut that sent him sprawling on his butt. Before he could get to his feet, she slammed her sneaker under his chin, holding down his neck.

Luckily Tim had never gotten his tighty whities off.

Tim coughed pathetically. She was crushing his windpipe.

"Get . . . off. . . ." He tried to talk but couldn't get

out the words. Keeping the pressure on his throat, Gaia bent at the waist and pulled up Tim's sleeves. There, practically glowing in the dim light, were three long, bloody scratches.

Gaia frowned with disgust. "We have a winner."

She pulled Mary's cell phone out of her pocket and dialed the local precinct. She only wished she could be there to see Mary's face when the call came through.

They were big,
but probably
slow. She
could deal,
but that would **the**
mean putting
sex
down the
ring
phone. And
just when
things were
getting good.

"GAIA, WHO THE HELL ARE YOU calling?" Tim asked, still pinned to the ground by her sneaker. The little diamond pattern on the sole was starting to make indentations in his neck. Gaia kind of liked it. Damn, she had a sick mind. "Can't we talk about—"

The Incompetents

He wheezed to a stop when Gaia pressed harder into his throat. She thought she heard him mutter the word *bitch*. There was no reason to let up if he was going to keep talking like that. Too annoying. The line rang twice, and then a gruff female voice answered the phone.

"Fifteenth Precinct." She sounded beyond bored, and there was the distinct crackle of popping gum.

"I need to talk to whatever detective is in with Mary Moss," Gaia said quickly, shoving her free hand in her pocket. She pulled out a wrapped peppermint. Something to get the Charlie taste out of her mouth.

"Oh, you do, do you?" the woman said, the grogginess leaving her voice as it was replaced by an edge of amusement. Gaia's request was apparently a good source of entertainment. "Detective Rodriguez is a very busy man. What makes you think you can just—"

"I have his perp or his collar or whatever," Gaia said, rolling her eyes. She looked down at Tim as if she just couldn't believe the incompetents at the police department. Tim lifted his head slightly and glared at her. He squirmed, but she didn't budge, so he cursed in defeat and slapped his head back onto the ground. Gaia unwrapped the mint and popped it into her mouth.

The woman on the other end of the line cleared her throat and then audibly shuffled through some papers. "Are you Gaia Moore?" she asked finally, sounding a bit chagrined.

"That's me," Gaia answered, rolling the candy around on her tongue.

There was a brief pause. A sigh. "He's expecting your call. I'll patch you through."

Gaia smiled slightly. It was kind of nice, being important among the incompetents. She looked up at the black sky while she waited on hold. Tim started to struggle a little, so she pushed down again, causing a strangled hacking sound to gurgle from his throat.

"Gaia?"

It was Charlie, along with a couple of friends, barreling out the back door. The wooden steps groaned like they wanted to buckle under the combined weight. Gaia checked them over to assess whether or not she could take them if they decided to defend their friend. They were big, but probably slow. She could deal, but that would mean putting down the

194

phone. And just when things were getting good.

"What do you think you're doing?" Charlie spat, his black eyes glimmering in the semidarkness. His raw-from-the-cold hands were clenched into fists.

"Charlie, thank Go—"

Gaia slammed her foot down again. She really had to pay more attention to keeping the captive silent.

The three guys lined up in front of her, holding their arms out slightly at their sides like a bunch of linebackers. Gaia could see their breath as it steamed from their mouths and noses in quick, short bursts. She could only hope they didn't know about Tim and his escapades. Maybe, just maybe, they'd be disgusted enough not to interfere.

"Sideburns Tim tried to rape me," Gaia said in a matter-of-fact tone. She held the phone out about an inch from her ear. "I'm in the process of turning him in."

A cloud of confusion settled onto Charlie's features, and he looked at his prone friend. His fists relaxed. "What?" he said, his brow a mass of wrinkles. "You . . . you tried to rape—"

In the middle of his sentence one of Charlie's sidekicks took off at a sprint, ripping open the back door so fast, he nearly took it off its hinges. Gaia heard a girl inside shout indignantly as he careened through the living room.

"Who was that?" she asked Charlie, raising her chin toward the back of the house.

"Chris Parker," Charlie answered, his face still drawn with shock.

"Detective Rodriguez," a voice snapped from the other end of the line.

"Yeah," Gaia said. "I have a rapist here by the name of Tim Racenello. And his accomplice is running up Horatio right now. His name's Chris Parker, and he has a really uneven buzz cut."

MARY GRINNED WHEN DETECTIVE Rodriguez picked up the phone and a surprised and indignant expression fell over his face like a curtain. He was definitely talking to Gaia. She was the only person in the world who inspired that exact reaction.

Safe

"Yes," the detective said, glancing at Mary from under his bushy eyebrows. "She's right here." He paused to listen and then turned in his chair so that one big, beefy shoulder was staring Mary in the face. She looked down at his gun in his leather shoulder holster, just below the ugly patch of sweat under his arm. She had a clear shot at the pistol. Not that she cared. But she wouldn't mind seeing his face if she stuck the barrel in it. He'd just spent fifteen minutes grilling her like she was the one who'd just kicked the shit out of someone for no reason.

"Yes, she told me the whole story," Rodriguez stage-whispered, his back hunching.

Not that he'd believed it.

"You have the perp there?" he asked, sitting back in his chair now. It creaked loudly in protest. Mary figured he'd decided there was no longer any point in keeping the truth from her. That her story was confirmed. That he was going to have to eat all his doubts with a shovel.

"We'll send someone over to pick him up," the detective said, making a few notes on a big yellow legal pad that was stained with old coffee rings. "Yes," he said, looking at Mary again. He almost looked like he wanted to hurt her. Some people just couldn't deal with being proven wrong. "Yes, I'll tell her." He paused and wiped a pudgy hand over his brow. "Thank you, Miss Moore."

He hung up the phone and let out a wet-sounding sigh, staring at the address he'd scrawled in front of him as he wiped his palms on his thighs.

"That's Ms.," Mary said with a cocky smile, tossing her curly red hair back from her face. The motion sent a pain through her skull, but she refused to wince.

"Huh?" Rodriguez asked.

"*Ms.* Moore," Mary repeated, crossing her arms over her chest and kicking out her legs. "You said Miss."

His face turned bright red, and for a second Mary thought he was going to reach out and strangle her, but a moment later he composed himself and ripped the page from his pad.

"Callahan!" he shouted, prompting a skinny little rookie in a pressed blue uniform to appear at his side like a hungry puppy. Rodriguez snapped the paper in the kid's face. "Take Robinson and go get this Racenello guy. He's at this address under the supervision of a Gaia Moore."

"Yes, sir," Callahan said, almost smiling as he took the paper and scurried off in search of his partner. Apparently this was a big thing for him. Mary hoped Gaia didn't give him any grief.

But it wasn't her problem. Her problem right now was that sometime in the next hour or so, she'd have to face the guy who attacked her. At least see him as he was dragged in. A big part of her didn't want to see his face. She didn't want to match a person with the animal that had attacked her. She didn't want to look into those eyes.

Mary leaned back in her uncomfortable chair, every bit of her body aching. Still, somehow she couldn't help smiling. Under the supervision of Gaia Moore.

She liked the sound of that.

Even after spending the last hour in the police station, it was the first moment she'd felt safe since the attack.

GAIA WATCHED, FEELING DETACHED,

Never Should Have Started

as the young officer pushed Tim's head down and half shoved him into the backseat of the squad car. It was the first real interaction she'd had with the police since the night Heather was slashed. The night everything about her was brought into question. The flashing red-and-blue lights should have signaled something good tonight. She'd caught the bad guy. Hopefully he'd be brought to justice.

Instead they just reminded her of what a general screwup she was. And she immediately thought of Sam.

He'd hated her after what happened to Heather. Had anything really changed since then? Was she ever going to know?

"Gaia?"

She glanced at the ground to her left and saw Charlie's scuffed-yet-expensive brown loafers next to her sneakers. Her stomach responded with an angry twist. She pulled her hands up inside the sleeves of her sweater and blew into the wool, warming her fingers as the car pulled away.

"What?" she asked finally, when she realized he wasn't going to speak again without being prompted. Like she felt like putting in the effort right now.

"I just wanted you to know I had no idea what was going on with him," Charlie said, shoving his hands into the back pockets of his jeans. "I swear I would never—"

"What you did was just as bad," Gaia said coldly, staring across the street at a decaying garbage can. She was totally disgusted with him, but she was sure that if she looked into his pleading eyes, she'd be even more sick. She couldn't believe she'd actually thought this guy could be a friend. That she took up for him to Ed.

Ed. Gaia squeezed her eyes shut. God, she was such an idiot. She'd defended a sex fiend to her one and only friend and practically called Ed a liar. She had some serious explaining to do. Pronto.

"What do you mean?" Charlie said now, sliding over so he was standing in front of her. He tilted his head down to catch her eye, making her look at him. He looked just like a puppy dog sitting under the table, begging for scraps. Gaia wanted nothing more than to kick him in the face. She would have, too, if the police weren't still milling around, asking questions. "I didn't try to force you. You know that."

"I know," Gaia said, a cold edge in her voice. She lifted her chin slightly and stared him down. "But you would have taken points for me."

The surprise in his face was highlighted by the sheer embarrassment. He took a step back, studying her warily as if she might be a witch or a psychic or something. "Who told you?" he asked.

"It doesn't matter," she said, pulling her jacket more tightly around her body. "I have somebody I have to see." She bowed her head and started up the street, steeling herself against the cold breeze.

"Gaia," he called after her.

"We're done talking, Charlie," she said, just loudly enough for him to hear. "We never should have started in the first place."

ELLA WAITED A GOOD FIVE MINUTES

A Wine— Worthy Victory

until she was sure Sam was gone. She'd never passed a more frustrating five minutes in her life. Every fiber of her being wanted to open the door, pull him inside, and seduce him as she so easily could.

But now wasn't the time. Not when she looked like a crazed lunatic and had just trashed her own house. Not her most attractive moment. Ella knew her limits.

Slowly she reached for the doorknob and pulled open the door. A little red box fell at her feet. Aw. A gift for Gaia. Ella almost puked from the sweetness of it all. She squatted with difficulty in her tight skirt and picked it up. When she shook it, it rattled noisily. Something with lots of pieces. Not jewelry. Sam obviously wasn't practiced in the art of wooing a girl. But then again, jewelry would be lost on Gaia. Almost everything of any importance was lost on Gaia.

Turning around, Ella whipped open the closet door and shoved the present way into the back. Behind her bagged furs and boxed hats. Behind all the stuff she'd never worn but absolutely had to have. She wasn't sure, at that moment, why she didn't just burn it. Destroy the evidence completely.

But knowing it was there was somehow comforting. It would be a silent reminder of the day she first triumphed over Gaia.

Something she would undoubtedly do many more times to come.

Ella laughed quietly as she closed the door with a click. Her stiletto heel ground into a piece of broken glass, and she surveyed her earlier damage with an amused glance. She could deal with that another time. She strolled into the office and sat down at the computer, hacking quickly into the e-mail account George had set up for Gaia.

Within five seconds she'd found an e-mail from Sam. One saying thanks for an interesting Thanksgiving. So that was how Gaia had found out. Well, things were about to get interesting in a whole new way.

Ella clicked the reply button and typed a quick e-mail. She snickered at her own creativity. But then, Gaia was so awkward, writing like her was easy.

It was almost too easy.

From: gaia13@alloymail.com
To: smoon@alloymail.com
Time: 9:05 P.M.
Re: re: Thanksgiving

Sam—

Thanks for the gift. You should know I have a boyfriend. From before. It's not going to happen between you and me. Sorry I didn't tell you before.

                                    —Gaia

When she was finished, Ella clicked send, then erased the e-mail from the list of sent mails so that Gaia wouldn't find it. Then she stood up and rubbed her hands together, feeling ever so much calmer than she had just fifteen minutes earlier.

This little victory definitely merited a glass of wine. Maybe even a large piece of cake.

Hell, she might even be nice to Gaia later.

In an alternate universe.

WITHOUT THE WIND, THE COLD WASN'T

so bad. It was almost re-
freshing. It gave Gaia a
chance to think. At first
when she'd left Charlie's,

Forgiveness

she'd been determined to go see Sam. She'd even made it
as far as the south end of the park. But when she'd looked
out at the shadows, looked ahead to the arch, she'd realized
there was something else she needed to do first.

Now, standing outside the apartment building, Gaia
felt almost calm. Almost at peace. She knew she
was where she was supposed to be. There was only one
person in this damn city who really cared about her.
Who'd put her in front of everyone else. A friend who
would hang out by the door every day just to see her face.

That is, if she hadn't totally destroyed the whole thing.

"Hey."

Gaia turned and looked into Ed's guarded brown eyes.

"I just came to say you were right, almost," Gaia
said quickly. "And I'm sorry."

The other amazing thing about Ed was it took him
only seconds to forgive her.

To: studentbody@villageschool.edu
Exclude: all males
From: shred@alloymail.com
Time: 9:05 P.M.
Re: payback

To whom it may concern:

There's a group of guys in our midst who have been taking advantage of many members of our female population. If you feel used, angry, even mildly dissatisfied with this randy group of partyers, meet us at the front office tomorrow morning at 8:30 sharp.

We'll help you get your revenge.

Rock on.

Shred

"My point is, ladies," he said, narrowing his eyes and looking them over **operation** as if **exposure** he were sizing up his platoon, "make your comments brief, and make them sting."

Goat Cheese

"FIRST OF ALL, I'D LIKE TO THANK everyone for coming," Ed said, maneuvering his chair in front of the group of five girls who had responded to his semicryptic schoolwide e-mail. He glanced up at Gaia, who stood as inconspicuously as possible with the others, and flashed her a smile. "I've managed to lie my way into approved use of the PA system for a few minutes this morning, but once the administration figures out what we're doing, you can bet they'll be banging down that door before you can say Operation Exposure."

He earned a few small laughs and giggles, so he paused to bask in the approval. Until Gaia grunted at him, eyeing the clock.

"My point is, ladies," he said, narrowing his eyes and looking them over as if he were sizing up his platoon, "make your comments brief, and make them sting."

He nodded at Gaia, who walked over to the door of the small auxiliary office and stood in front of it like a bouncer at a bar on Canal Street. For now they had the room to themselves, but Gaia was their only line of defense should Principal Hickey decide to come barging in. She wasn't going to beat him up or anything, but she did have some delay tactics in mind. Ones she wouldn't share with Ed, of course.

"Who's up first?" Ed asked, glancing at each of five wary faces. Chrissy Margolis bit her lip and glanced at the others, then stood, pulling down on her batik print skirt.

"I'll go," she said, her face disturbingly pale.

Ed smiled reassuringly, picked up the PA mike, and flipped the switch. The clock read 8:42 A.M. Just about the entire student body should be milling around the halls right now, exchanging last minute homework and gabbing about last night's *Friends* plot. It was perfect timing.

"Can I have your attention, please?" Ed recited into the microphone. "My name is Ed Fargo, and I'm here to talk to you about a very insidious plague that's running rampant in our school. It calls itself the Stud Club, if you can believe it, and the guys who hold memberships think they're pretty damn suave." He glanced over at Gaia, who rolled her eyes but was obviously concentrating to keep from smiling. "But I have some women here who would like to set the record straight," Ed finished.

Looking up at Chrissy's face, Ed had a sudden logic flash. "You'll understand in a moment why I choose to withhold their names."

As he handed the microphone up to Chrissy, her expression was all about relief. She lifted her chin, tossed back her curly hair, and cleared her throat.

"I'd just like everyone to know that Josh Talbot loses more saliva when he kisses than my dog produces in a year."

208

The girls behind her laughed, and she handed the microphone off to Gina Waters, who suddenly looked like she had attitude to spare. Ed wouldn't want to be on the receiving end of this one. Gina grasped the microphone as if it were a relay race baton, her knuckles turning white as she brought the mike to her mouth.

"My message is for Charlie Salita. Charlie, my friend, you last about as long as a biscuit in a dog kennel."

She bowed to the applause from the peanut gallery and gave the mike to a scrawny little girl who couldn't have been more than a freshman. It made Ed's stomach twist in a hundred directions to think someone had taken advantage of a girl so frail.

She cleared her throat demurely before speaking. "Charlie Salita . . . ," she said, smirking slightly and looking up at Gina, "wouldn't know what to do with his tongue if it came with an instruction manual."

Gina let out a cheer of approval and high-fived the girl, who was giggling crazily at her own audacity. Gaia even cracked a smile, and Ed couldn't help thinking that it looked like Gaia was agreeing with the frosh. So she *had* kissed Charlie. Ick. Ed's life couldn't possibly get more unfair.

The freshman held the microphone out at the same instant the doorknob started to rattle. Ed's heart jumped and started racing at a pace that couldn't possibly be healthy. He shot Gaia a questioning look.

"Keep going," Gaia said, glancing at the lock. "They definitely have a key."

"When Chris Parker isn't sucking in, he has a gut that small children could use as a trampoline," the next girl said quickly, her eyes flashing with triumph as she passed on the mike.

Ed could hear the jangling of an overstuffed key ring outside the office door. His heart was in his throat. At this point lifelong detention was a given—he just wanted all of the girls to get in their insults before they got busted.

Mara Trauth grabbed the microphone, watching the door from the corner of her eye. It started to open, and Gaia grabbed the knob, slamming it closed again and using all her weight to pull against it. "Come on," Gaia urged through clenched teeth.

"That's your delay tactic?" Ed hissed, glaring at her.

"Now you understand why I didn't want to share it," Gaia deadpanned.

Ed turned his attention to Mara, who didn't seem to be breathing. "Um . . . uh . . ."

He hit full panic mode when he realized she was shaking and her hands were sweating profusely. She looked at him wide-eyed, like she was asking for help, but Ed had no idea what he could do for her.

"It's okay," he said, going for the calming-guidance-counselor tone. "Just say whatever comes to your mind."

Swallowing hard, Mara took in a shaky breath. "Dan Swarski smells like year-old goat cheese."

Her brow knitted, and she looked at Ed. "Was that okay?"

Ed nodded with a grin just as the door flew open and Principal Hickey burst in with his army of Village School rent-a-cops. The man looked like he'd just eaten a plateful of red-hot chili peppers.

"My office," he said with a growl. "Now."

They were big-time busted, but as Ed looked around at the gratified faces of the women around him, he knew it was worth it.

He only wished Heather had joined in on the fun.

HEATHER LICKED THE TIP OF HER

Waiting for Ed

pinky and smoothed the end of her left eyebrow, leaning in close to the scratched-up mirror in the school bathroom. As always, her exterior was calm and flawless, but inside, her heart was pounding like a dance club bass beat.

And for the first time in ages, it was because she was waiting for Ed.

She had something she needed to say to him, and just thinking about what he'd done that morning—what he'd done for her—made her pulse do strange things. So here she was, hovering in the deserted bathroom across the way from the detention hall, waiting for Ed without looking like she was waiting for him.

When she heard his wheelchair in the hall, her breath caught momentarily, and she shook her head at her reflection. There was definitely something wrong with her. Something deep-seated and possibly pathological. But there was no use analyzing it. Right now, she had a mission.

Shaking her hair back from her face, Heather swung open the door and walked out into the hallway just before Ed turned his chair into the detention hall. What a coincidence.

"Heather," Ed said. She was sure there was a hint of excitement in his voice. Just a tad.

"Ed," she said, totally surprised to see him. "What's up?" She smoothed down the front of her white button-down shirt and half smiled.

"Nothing," Ed said, glancing into the classroom. He moved down the hall slightly, out of sight of anyone inside, and Heather followed. "How are you?" Ed asked.

"I'm okay," Heather said nonchalantly. "Listen, I've been meaning to thank you for what you did this morning," she said in a whisper.

Ed grinned. "Charlie really got the brunt of it, didn't he?" he said, completely satisfied with himself.

Heather smirked and crossed her arms over her chest. "Yeah, he did." Her heart was still racing, and it brought a blush to her face. She was heading into dangerous territory. If he noticed anything was different about her, there would be no going back. "So, anyway," she said. "Thanks. For everything."

"You're welcome," Ed said seriously, lacing his fingers together in front of him. "I didn't do it for you, you know," he said, a flash of mischief in his eyes.

Heather smiled back. "Yeah, I know," she said with a laugh. "I'll see ya," she said, and turning on her heel, she started off down the hall, her head holding itself high for the first time all week.

She knew exactly why Ed had done what he did. Why he'd gone to all that trouble to round up those girls and give them a chance to skewer the assholes who had used them. The assholes who had used *her*. He'd done it because he was a good person. And he had a good heart.

And because he still cared about her.

GAIA HAD ACTUALLY LEFT SCHOOL

feeling pretty damn good about herself. Not only had she helped Ed ex-
pose the Stud Club boys that
morning, but she'd not had one evil
thought about Heather all day, and
she'd spent the entire time in detention thinking solely in

A Little Red Box

Russian. All in all, in Gaia terms, it was a perfect school
day.

But by the time she walked up the steps at George
and Ella's that evening, Gaia was back on self-
deprecation mode. And it was all Sam Moon's fault.

Okay, so she wasn't exactly experienced in this
stuff, but she hadn't stopped obsessing about
Thanksgiving once since he'd e-mailed her. Well, except for those brief moments of focused hatred on
Charlie and Tim and beating the crap out of people.

Gaia sighed as she closed the heavy wooden door
behind her. She leaned back against its cool surface
and stared at the foyer. Didn't he know that a person
couldn't send a cryptic e-mail like that and not follow
up on it? Didn't he know what he was
putting her through?

"You're being a whiny girl, Gaia," she told herself,
pushing away from the door. "You're annoying me."

After all, she hadn't contacted him, either. Yeah,
she'd skulked around the park, staked out his dorm,

triple checked her e-mail, but she hadn't called him or written to him or buzzed his room. This was an equal opportunity nonrelationship.

Gaia pulled her messenger bag off over her head and dropped it on the floor under the now conspicuously empty hall table. She briefly wondered what Ella had done with all her hideous knickknacks but then decided not to waste brain space on it. She should just count herself lucky they were gone and hope they weren't replaced by something even more ceramic-y and pink.

Opening the door to the closet, Gaia automatically reached for the empty hanger she always left behind, but her hand hit a nylon jacket instead. She looked at the rack and groaned. Someone had taken her hanger. She opened the door wider and started to search, pushing aside a few of Ella's musty fur coats until she found a bent and abused wire hanger.

As she fought to pull it out, her eyes fell on a little red box stuffed onto a shelf between a hatbox and a stack of old magazines. Gaia just looked at it for a moment, wondering if it was some Christmas gift for George from Ella. She could just imagine the kind of present Ella would buy for her husband. Probably a copy of *Eight-Minute Abs* or one of those spray-on hair kits.

Gaia rolled her eyes, slung her jacket over the hanger, and slammed the closet door.

She was sure she wouldn't be getting anything for Christmas this year, at least not from her dad or her uncle or anyone who mattered. But as she grabbed her bag and trudged up the stairs, she realized she didn't really want gifts, anyway.

As pathetic as it was, all she wanted was for Sam to call.

THE PHONE WAS RINGING WHEN SHE

walked into her bedroom, and she dropped her things onto her bed, diving for the receiver.

"Hello?" she said, breathless after climbing about a million stairs. She sprawled out on her stomach across her comforter.

Sam's Call

"Hey."

Her heart skipped crazily, and she rolled over onto her back, a slow smile spreading across her face.

"I was wondering if I'd ever hear from you," she said.

"I know," he said slowly. "I'm sorry it's been a while. You don't know how sorry."

"That's okay," Heather said, grinning for real. "I'm just happy to hear your voice."

DON'T MISS
FEARLESS #7
REBEL
COMING NEXT MONTH
FROM POCKET PULSE

FEARLESS™

**Gaia's fearless.
Now do you want to
test your own fear gene?**

Register to win a Fearless™ Vacation.

Alloy and the cool peeps at Adventure Treks
are giving you the chance to rock climb,
backpack, whitewater raft, sleep under the
stars - your chance to have a rad experience.

It's not for the faint of heart.
Think you've got what it takes?

Then check out

www.alloy.com

for your chance to win.

FEARLESS™

OFFICIAL RULES FOR
"WIN A FEARLESS VACATION AT ALLOY.COM"

NO PURCHASE NECESSARY. Sweepstakes begins February 1, 2000 and ends March 31, 2000. Entrants must be 14 years or older as of February 1, 2000 and a legal U.S. resident to enter. Corporate entities are not eligible. Employees and the immediate family members of such employees (or people living in the same household) of Alloy Online, Inc., Simon & Schuster, Inc., and 17th Street Productions, Adventure Treks and their respective advertising, promotion, production agencies and the affiliated companies of each are not eligible. Participation in this Sweepstakes constitutes contestant's full and unconditional agreement to and acceptance of the Official Sweepstakes Rules.

HOW TO ENTER: To enter, visit the Alloy Web site at www.alloy.com. Submit your entry by fully completing the entry form at the site. Entries must be received by March 31, 2000, 11:59 p.m., Eastern Standard Time. There is no charge or cost to register. No mechanically reproduced entries accepted. One entry per e-mail address. Simon & Schuster, Inc., Alloy Online, Inc., Adventure Treks and their respective agents are not responsible for incomplete, lost, late, damaged illegible or misdirected e-mail or for technical, hardware or software failures of any kind, lost or unavailable network connections, or failed, incomplete garbled or delayed computer transmissions which may limit a user's ability to participate in the Sweepstakes. All notifications in the Sweepstakes will be sent by e-mail. Sponsor is not responsible, and may disqualify you if your e-mail address does not work or if it is changed without prior notice to us via e-mail at contest@alloymail.com. Sponsor reserves the right to cancel or modify the Sweepstakes if fraud or technical failures destroy the integrity of the Sweepstakes as determined by Sponsor, in its sole discretion. If the Sweepstakes is so canceled, announced winner will receive prize to which s/he is entitled as of the date of cancellation.

RANDOM DRAWING: Prize Winner will be selected in a random drawing from among all eligible entries on April 1, 2000 to be conducted by Alloy Online designated judges, whose decisions are final. Winner will be notified by e-mail on or about April 3, 2000. Odds of winning the prize depends on the number of eligible entries received.

PRIZE:(1): A free trip for one on an Adventure Treks trip (specific trip to be chosen by Adventure Treks/Alloy) redeemable during summer 2000. Trip duration approximately 2–4 weeks. (Approximate retail value: $4,000)

FEARLESS™

Prize is subject to all federal, state and local taxes, which are the sole responsibility of the winner. Prizes are not transferable. No cash substitution, transfer or assignment of prize will be allowed, except by Sponsor in which case a prize of equal or greater value will be awarded.

GENERAL: All federal, state and local laws and regulations apply. Void in Florida, Puerto Rico and wherever prohibited by law. By entering, winner or if applicable winner's parent or legal guardian consents to use of winner's name by Sponsor without additional compensation. Entries become Sponsor's property and will not be returned. For a copy of these official rules, send a self-addressed stamped envelope to Alloy 115 West 30th Street #210, NY, NY 10001, Attn: Fearless Vacation Sweepstakes.

AFFIDAVIT OF ELIGIBILTY/RELEASE: To be eligible to win, winner will be required to sign and return an affidavit of eligibility/release of liability (except where prohibited by law). Winner under the age of 18 must have their parent or guardian sign the affidavit and release as well. Failure to sign and return the affidavit or release within 14 days, or to comply with any term or condition in these Official Rules may result in disqualification and the prize being awarded to an alternate winner. Return of any-prize notification/prize as undeliverable may result in disqualification and the awarding of the prize to an alternate winner. By accepting prize, winner grants Sponsor permission to use his or her name, picture, portrait, likeness and voice for advertising, promotional and/or publicity purposes connected with this Sweepstakes without additional compensation (except where prohibited by law).

Neither Simon & Schuster, Inc., 17th Street Productions, nor Sponsor shall have responsibility or liability for any injury, loss or damage of any kind arising out of participation in this Sweepstakes or the acceptance or use of the prize.

WINNER: The winner's first name and state of residence will be posted at www.alloy.com on April 10, 2000 or, for the winner's name and state of residence available after April 15, 2000, send a self-addressed, stamped, #10 envelope to: Alloy 115 West 30th Street #201 NY, NY 10001, Attn: Fearless Vacation Sweepstakes.